Wandering Journey and the Collapsing Castles

CHAPTER ONE

In a warm morning of a sunny day at the end of March of 1958, Muhajer was constructing the miniature building of his imaginary house in the shade of a carob tree in his father's olive grove. He was a six-year-old chubby boy with a soiled reddish brown dishdasha_ a short garment that had taken its color from the dark reddish soil of the ground he would sit on. He would spend most of his time playing in the shade of the old trees of the grove. His garment was full of patches: brown, red, white, and black. The original color of the fabric of the dishdasha was light brown, but the color faded away and the garment was worn to shreds as time passed by. Whenever the boy's garment needed mending, Rifqa, the boy's mother, would mend it with any obtainable rag regardless of its color. The garment's lower edge was worn and shredded, too. The child looked miserable as if he had been living with his enemies. Out of his two eyes, two dark strings were sliding down his pale cheeks as if they were two dry rivers of sorrow and grief bespeaking the miserable life he was leading. The strings were the traces of the tears that would flow down his cheeks when he was hit or punished by his parents. He would weep for long hours after being beaten by one of his parents! They treated him ruthlessly. They would punish him severely believing that the harsh treatment would make him a tough man who would withstand adversities and challenges of his future life as a villager in that isolated place.

The boy was collecting small stones and gravels to build his miniature house. It was a warm morning. The sun was ascending in the sky over the shimmering remote mountains of Trans- Jordan in the east. To the far left end of those mountains, at the far horizon was the summit of Mount Harmon with its snow caped peak piercing the low white strata clouds? In the remote plain in the valley were vast ponds supposed to be fisheries. To the east of those fisheries was the Jordan River which looked like a huge startled snake winding with its glittering water running from the north to the south, flowing through two parallel rows of thick cinchona, and green willow trees. The dark green trees growing on the two edges of the river looked like parallel high hedges flanking the bed of the river. .

The grove was located on the highest peak of the chain of hills flanking the Jordan valley from the west. The landscape was fabulous. The valley down there looked very captivating with glittering surfaces of water and the dark green trees that cover a wide landscape. Reflecting the sunrays, the ponds looked like huge glittering mirrors. They captured the attention of the little boy who asked his mother: "what are those things?" She answered: "They are fisheries. They produce fish." The child had never seen a fish. He did not understand her answer, but he wanted to know more and asked another question; "Whom do they belong to?" She angrily said: " Listen, you! son of the accursed parents, I do not know! They belong to many people who can encircle the whole Earth. Shut up and ask your father when he comes back."

The world to Rifqa, the boy's mother, ended at the horizons that she could see, where the sky met the ground: To the west were high mountains that the sun disappeared behind every night. To the east were the mountains of Transjordan where the sun always rose every morning. Between the west and the east ridges of mountains was the Jordan valley (El-Aghwar). To the north were the remote mountains that Rifqa could hardly see.

At the horizon to the south there were rows of wild trees growing at the peaks of high hills.

The child was puzzled by his mother's harsh answer! He felt resentful. His mother had never tolerated his actions nor his questions that were always answered by" I don't know, shut up!" Yesterday she whipped his little back twenty times ruthlessly, saturating his garment with blood emanating out of the lesions inflected by frequent flogging of his back.

That morning, he felt the pain every time he moved his right hand to pick a stone! The torment was very severe and Muhajer was expecting more of it. The bad treatment annoyed the child terribly: He had become resentful and inclined to mutiny and stubbornness; He began to pretend that he did not hear well. He would not respond to the callings of people around him unless someone shouted to him. Life was bitter for him, the food he ate and the water he drank always tasted bitter.

Then, the boy kicked his younger sister, making her fall to the ground. The mother ran up to them saying: "May Allah break your arms," kicking his head with her shoe. The child burst into crying. His sister, Haleemah, ran towards him. When she was near enough to him, he pushed her with his two hands, saying:" Go away!" The little girl who was at the beginning of her fifth year fell to the ground crying. Rifqa said loudly:" May Allah break your hands! You son of the perished, damn you and damn the day I saw you!" Then, she took a long lean limb of a carob tree and hit the back of the boy heavily several times. Therefore, he screamed loudly. His shrill cries reverberated throughout the dales and valleys around the grove. The back of his dishdashah was stained with small drops of blood dotted through the cloth.

The boy insisted that his mother help him cut the carob limbs for the ceiling of his make-believe house! Rifqa asked: "Why are you building this house? Do you want to live in it?" The boy thought for a while; he realized that it was only a fantasy house, he could not enter, nor could he live therein.

He looked at her saying: "The house that I will build when I become a man will be like this house. I will build a beautiful house better than yours at the hamlet!" Rifqa was baffled to hear the boy's answer; she said: "I wish God shortened your life. God willing, you will not become a grown up man. I wish Allah took you soon!"

The boy felt dejected and frustrated; Tears were running down his cheeks. He asked: "Why do you not love me? Aren't you my mother?"

Because of the unfair treatment by his parents, the child would weep for long hours! His complexion revealed the miserable life and reflected the adverse conditions under which he was living. The tears that would flow down his cheeks left traces like two strings flowing down from his eyes: they were two dry rivers of grief and sadness running down his cheeks.

Rifqa commented: "You are a wicked boy! You are not my son, you are the son of the gypsies; they lost you in the heath and we found you there! You were a bad omen when you came to me." The boy said; "When the gypsies come in the summer. I will go to them and say that I am their son! So they will take me with them!" Now, Rifqa said: "Shut up! Stop it! Don't talk." She hit him with a leather type steel toed boot, but it missed him this time." The boy said; "O.K., you are not my mother, you are not my parents! I will leave you tonight and go out into the darkness so that the wild beasts will kill me. I wish that a hyena killed me tonight." Rifqa, was upset with the boy's behavior that hindered her work. She could not tolerate the boy's screams that reverberated throughout the whole place with its dales and valleys. So, she kicked him with her right foot and sent him rolling down a steep slope covered with the thorny bushes of poterium spinosum the thorns of which pierced the skin of the little child. The child kept rolling down the slope until he settled by the stone chain which was the   border that separated the grove from the adjacent groves. The chain of stones encircled the grove separating it from the adjacent groves.

Hadjis , Muhajer's father, had planted some cactus(prickly pear) trees along the stony wall , forming an inside wall with their broad prickly thick leaves . It was difficult to enter the grove except through openings that Hadjis made for this purpose. The main gate was at the end of the eastern wall that met the southern wall. It was a wide opening that animals and people could pass through easily

x

The child was terrified and he stayed there sobbing. The boy noticed a rattlesnake peeping at him through a hole beneath a rock. So, he shouted loudly: "Snake! Snake!" Rifqa hurried to him. He pointed with his right index to the hole beneath a flat rock. Rifqa did not see the snake. She ruthlessly kicked Muhajer's head with her right foot, wearing an old heavy boot. The boy assured her that he saw a snake whose color was similar to the color of the soil there! She brought an old rubber shoe and she set fire to it at the opening of the hole in order to smother the snake therein

A few minutes later, the girl shouted: "Snake! Snake!" Rifqa noticed the snake sliding on a flat smooth rock protruding near the stone chain and she violently threw a rock at the snake cutting it into two pieces_ one of them with the head of the snake still intact. She held a heavy stick and smashed the head of the snake! They boy was pleased with his mother's action. He hurried to his mother, kissed her right hand, and begged her not to tell his father about his naughtiness but she refused. He went on crying and shouting frantically. "To hell with you! May Allah (God) shorten your life! Stop it! Stop it! I've got work to do!" Rifqa shouted!

A few minutes later, silence prevailed over the place, but down the hill along the track winding across the slope of a bushy hill, a ghost-like man was beating a donkey loaded with two olive colored metal containers, or gallons as the villagers used to call them, though each container took more than twenty liters of water. He was beating the donkey to make him move faster! The containers were used for transporting water filled from sources of water like springs or cisterns that were designed by the villagers to collect the rainwater during winter. Hadjis had a good stature, his face was sunburnt; his eyes were like a hawk eyes. His nose was curved. He looked like a hawk. He looked fearful when angry. He was at the beginning of his forties, ten years older than his wife Rifqa, who was in her thirties.

When Hadjis arrived at the cavern, he went to see whether Rifqa had finished digging the ground around some trees. He was shocked to see that his wife had not finished the digging that she was supposed to do during his absence. He was very angry and this anger intensified his first anger when he was down there walking behind the donkey: he heard the boy's creaming. He was upset, because he knew well Rifqa's harsh treatment of the child.

Noticing that she did not finish the work, Hadjis was enraged, but without uttering any words, he kicked her violently with his heavy boots and sent her rolling down the steep slope. Settling down by the border wall of stones where the boy had been lying, she was surprised to see the boy become happy at her wretchedness! She said: "Damn you and damn the day you came to me! Are you pleased now? Your father broke my ribs with his boots! "

The boy laughed. So, she said:" You! Son of a bitch! Your parents are damned! You are the root cause of my wretchedness." She slapped his face twice! At this moment, Hadjis came down to the them and began shouting": You bitch! Why did you not finish the digging? You were playing with this bastard building his house! What a little mind you have?" The boy said: "she hit me with a stick, look at my back. It is full of blood! She said to me that I am not your child, you found me in the heath. The gypsies lost me there. You are not my parents, both of you! "To this, Hadjis looked horrified and he addressed Rifqa:" Well! Well! You want to expose me and send me to jail! You bitch, you want to send me to jail; you want to expose us! Why did you say that to him?"

Sobbing, Rifqa tried to silence the boy. She said: "I was not serious! Just I wanted to appease him: he was crying and shouting. I have finished digging the ground of five trees and the sixth I had not finished as this monkey was crying and shouting. You did not notice the other five remote olive seedlings you planted last year around the huge flat rock beyond the oldest carob tree. This black-faced boy caused a lot of trouble to me! He hindered my work."

Then, Hadjis grabbed the boy by the collar of his dishdasha , lifted him up high above his head , and threw him violently to the ground leaving him naked as his grip tore the boy's dress. It was torn off and it remained with its collar in Hadjis 's hand! It was very old worn ragged dress. The boy was left naked. Hadjis went directly to the boy's almost finished miniature house and scooped its tiny stony walls with a shovel and hurled them unto the stony border : the pebbles were scattered over the rock border ; most of them fell beyond the wall. Therefore, the boy was terrified. He saw his dream evaporate when he could defend neither himself nor his little house. Meanwhile, Haleema was terrified; she felt insecure as she was afraid that her father might beat her as he would do when he lost his temper!

The boy started crying loudly. Hadjis shouted to Rifqa to silence the boy or he would break his neck. Rifqa brought an old dishdasha for the boy to wear. It was black like his face she said.

The boy was between the devil and blue seas, both parents were angry with him and they were ruthless; it seemed that they were looking for a way to get rid of him. The boy was thirsty and he asked for some water, but both parents refused to give him water. So, he perched on his knees and arms on the ground and pretended that he was asleep among the high grass there! A few minutes later, while his parent were busy weeding the grass beneath the olive trees, he crept through the thorny bushes heading for the little squirt of water that was trickling down on the surface of a smooth white wide flat rock in the southern part of the olive grove. The water would collect in a little hole that Hadjis had dug in the surface of a flat rock to collect the water of the squirt dripping from beneath a huge rock there. When the water overfilled the hole which could take two to three liters of water, it would flow down the rock, which was slanted towards an olive tree that was a few feet away. Therefore, that tree grew faster than the other seedlings and it outgrew the trees around. The boy found the hole full of water to the brim. The water was very cool He scooped with the palms of both hands some water and began to drink. The water collecting in that hole was not enough for the needs of the family and their animals. So, Hadis had to go daily to the far sources of water to bring water for the family needs.

The boy saw that there was a shepherd sleeping on the huge smooth flat rock, which was shattered by the trunk of an old gnarled olive tree sprouting there; the trunk of the tree had rifted the rock apart and the boy could hide in the rift. But he noticed that there were black goats devouring the newly sprouting green twigs of the olive trees. So he ran towards the north where his parents were. As he was at the highest spot of the slope far away from the goats, he began shouting to his father: "Goats! Goats! "

As the child was shouting to his father, Hadjis heard the ringing of the goat bells. So he abruptly said to Rifqa: "I will later make sure of what you say". He jumped up carrying a shovel as he heard the boy's shouting as well as the ringing of the bells of some goats at the other side of the grove. He went running. He saw the perilous ravenous enemy of the olive trees_ goats! While he was approaching, he tiptoed briskly not causing any sounds lest he should draw the attention of the shepherd. As he got there, he saw the shepherd sleeping in the shade of a high huge olive tree ; he was fast asleep ,letting his goats devour the dry grass as well as the mellow leaves of the olive tree twigs , the newly sprouting twigs! At this moment, Hadjis shouted: " Damn you and damn your parents, "striking the head of the shepherd with the blade of the shovel! Blood gushed out of the frontal skin of the shepherd who was fast asleep. Hit with the shovel, the boy sprang up to his feet crying: "please, Afendi! please Afendi !I am in your face!(I seek your protection!): don't beat me I'll never ever come to this place again!"

Rifqa hurried to the scene! The shepherd's frontal skin was bleeding heavily. "Bring some water!" shouted Hadjis . The woman brought the water. Hadis put some coffee powder on the open cut and bandaged the boy's bleeding head with the soiled white scarf of the boy and let him go! The boy let his goats loose and hurried down the hill going back for the hamlet. As he was about two hundred yards away, he tumbled over a dry trunk of an old uprooted olive tree .He cried loudly but he rose up. He could hardly drag his feet. He dragged himself down the slope leading to the low plain adjoining the grove hill, it was among three hills. In that plain, there were some black tents for some people of the hamlet. Among them was the shepherd family tent.

No sooner, had he got to the tents than a band of a dozen young men emerged from the tents shouting and calling Hadjis names. To this, Hadjis swiftly ran for the cavern! He fetched a Lee Enfield rifle and fired warning shots in the air. In time, a number of men of Hadjis 's clan arrived riding their horses and they dispersed the band of the young men who were going to attack Hadjis !. The horse men of Hadjis's clan hurried to the grove in response to the shots they heard. Firing shots in the air meant a call for help.

Next day, Hadjis was summoned to the police station at Munqatta'a in Al Aghwar! The police force there consisted of eight equestrians .They were the terror of the region. To avoid the police officers harsh treatment, the villagers themselves amicably settled their conflicts. Complaining to the police station was very costly. It would cost the complainant nearly half a dozen of his goats or sheep and, let alone all of his/her hens that were completely vanished off earth because all of them would be sacrificed for the banquets and meals for the equestrians. Therefore, "it was better to bow for the aggressor than losing a wealth for the arbiter."

When Hadjis arrived at the station, the commander, of the force ordered his men to put his feet in the Falaka position and give him the bamboo canes. Realizing that it would be a severe corporal punishment, Hadjis mustered his courage and shouted": Hold it! You cannot beat me! I am a soldier like you! I am a reserve soldier and here is my I.D." So, the sergeant asked them not to beat him and he summoned him to his office for cross- examination. Hadjis remarked that he knew the reason for the police harsh treatment. He said: "I know the reason of your severe corporal punishment of the people summoned to the station and the outlaws who happened to fall in your hands. You act harshly, I believe, because you want to create the impression that there is no leniency for the outlaws." The sergeant laughed and said that he was pleased to see a brave reserve soldier like him and he promised Hadjis to sympathize with him, because the sergeant himself would encourage people to plant their land with trees.

The commander of the police station released Hadjis , giving him a notice summoning the shepherd and his father to the police station the next day. But, the boy and his father did not show up. Therefore, two equestrians were sent to fetch them both to the police station! The hamlet was ten kilometers away from the station.

The appearance of the police equestrians would create a state of panic among the inhabitants, especially, the villagers. While those two men were riding their horses heading for the hamlet, a peasant saw them approaching the field of sorghum he was guarding with a hand sling; he would stand on a bower of wood among the stalks of the sorghum field and use his sling for hurling small stones to terrify the birds away. The guard hid among the tall stalks of sorghum.

When the two equestrians reached the sorghum field, one of them noticed that there was no body on the bower to frighten the birds. So he said to his colleague:" I think the man who is guarding the field is hiding among the stalks. I will call out: Hey! You hiding there, I can see you come out or I will fire at you. " No sooner had he uttered his words than a man with a terrified complexion appeared and timidly said: ; "I am in your faces!"(I seek your protection!). Treat me kindly. I did not mean to hide from you!" The two men burst into laughing, let him go, and resumed their journey.

When the two equestrians arrived at the hamlet, a wave of panic swept over the place. Men gathered at the house of the shepherd welcoming the two equestrians. Two fatty sheep were slaughtered and cooked to honor the knights as guests. In the afternoon, they took the goat boy with them; he was walking in front of the horses.

Two days later, the sergeant of the force went with three of his men taking the shepherd (the goat boy) with them to the hamlet to settle the problem amicably. The majority of the men of the hamlet gathered in a huge black hosting tent with a large compartment that would take in sixty or seventy men. Colorful mattresses with embroiled cushions were spread in the tent in a rectangular shape in the middle of the rectangle of the tent that had its curtains raised. There were three main poles at intervals of four meters in the middle of the tent where there was a hole for fire with three pots of coffee over a wire grill stuck on the fire. There were gentle west breezes blowing at the time. The floor of the tent was furnished with colorful Arabian hand woven rugs. This tent was the hosting tent. Some men went directly there, and a few young men kindled the fire for making Arabian coffee. Other young men were busy: they killed seven sheep for honoring the guests.

Fire was kindled in the hole in front of the tent for making coffee, the three coffee pots were always handy. They were black with successive use on fire of wood logs. But the pot for serving the coffee was always polished with brass and it was always shining with its golden color.

Coffee was served. The first cup of coffee was handed to the commander who put it down! Following the predominant Arabian custom, he did not drink it before having a positive response to his request.

The headman of the hamlet realized that the commander had a request: so he said: "Drink your coffee and your request will be met, God willing." The commander said he had no personal request, but he came to settle the problem of Hadjis and the shepherd. He added that the generous hospitality with which he and his men were received with encouraged him to proceed with the task he came to accomplish. The commander said that the natives are noble men as he noticed! The generosity of the hamlet's inhabitants indicated they were of a noble ancestry and he hoped that the problem be solved amicably instead of taking it to court. If it were taken to court, the two parties would lose much. Hadjis said that he would accept a compromise and the other party consented, too.

The sergeant asked Hadjis to present his argument. Hadjis said: "Sir, 1 am a poor man and I don't have many arable units of land as others do. I have only a small grove of olive besides other areas of land far away from the hamlet. Last year, I planted a few olive seedlings to have a new generation of olive trees. I brought them from the groves of the nearby villages in order to improve the quality of the olive products of my grove. This boy and his father with his uncles always take their goats into my grove and let them destroy the newly planted seedlings. So far, they have destroyed about two hundred trees. I want them to recompense the loss for me and undertake that they shall never harm my trees again."

The sergeant, then, asked the boy to bring forth his argument: The boy said that Hadjis assaulted him without alerting him. He almost broke his skull.

Then, the sergeant delivered a speech. He urged the two parties to tolerate, respect, and honor one another. He said that solving problem amicably is better than having solved by the force of law. An amicable solution is better than imposed solutions. He suggested that Hadjis hold a banquet in honor of the goat boy and his father while the goat boy and his father should recompense Hadjis for the two hundred trees that they destroyed- a dinar per a tree! The boy's father protested that suggestion would cost him a fortune! He haughtily added that he would not accept that settlement. Therefore, the sergeant firmly addressed the shepherd's father: "Hold your horses! You have to go with us to our station and you will be detained there until the court takes a decision."

At this moment, the hamlet's headman intervened: "May I say a word, sergeant? Please don't take him with you, we know how he will be treated there with your honorable bamboo canes that would gently lash his calves." The audience burst into laughing though the boy and his father were utterly stumped by the headman's comment. They realized well what might happen! The headman added that a compromise could be reached! Hadjis had never rejected any of his suggestions. He suggested that the boy and his father give 50 dinars to Hadjis for the damages of his olive trees. The two parties consented to the headman's suggestion and they stood up shaking their hands and reciprocated kissing the beards of one another, indicating the end of their dispute!

Then, the sergeant asked the headman:" How do know that the strokes of bamboo canes are painful?" The headman said: "Experience is the teacher of fools!" I learned through experience. Most of the people present, here, know my story! The sergeant curiosity was aroused; he wanted to learn more. So he asked:" Have you ever had a corporal punishment by our horsemen?" The headman said it was along tale, but he would tell it in short. He said: "It happened in the summer of 1947. On August 14, the elderly of the hamlet elected me as the headman: The next day was the middle of August, that is, it was very hot. When the sun was in the middle of sky, the temperature reached its highest point; if you filled a plate with water and left it in the sun, it would evaporate very soon. Suddenly we noticed a British patrol approaching the hamlet. They were looking for an outlaw!

When they arrived at the hamlet; they were swimming in sweat: Their uniforms were soaked with sweat. Their faces were red especially their noses. They were very exhausted because of the heat. Moreover, the road was rugged; they were very nervous because of the unbearably hot journey. Among them, their commander was the most nervous. They began to ask people in English. Nobody understood in the village understood English. Some young men hurried to me and asked me to meet the commander of the patrol. The inhabitants, then, believed that I spoke English very well because they thought that I had learnt English well when I was detained for five years by the British mandate authorities in Palestine. In fact, I learned very few words. I went forward to the officer and said, "Hi! Mr. Fucking. So, he at once responded: 'Fucking Arab! Fucking Arab!' He began beating my two leg calves with his bamboo cane. The lashes stung my calves the strokes were like scorpion stings. They were very painful so I screeched out of pain." I had a very painful experience on the first day I assumed my position as a headman! So if Abu Salem, the boy's father, rejects your settlement, then invite him to try the taste of the strokes of your bamboo canes! The sergeant and the crowd burst into laughing: The sergeant commented:" you cursed the man rather than welcoming him"

The headman said: "I thought it was the best greeting phrase I had learned. The imperialists colonize your country, but they do not benefit you. They do not educate you properly. I returned their goods to them. "If you search this hamlet you will never find a radio set there. I have convinced the inhabitants that those radio sets only receive bad news and bring evil. The land and the people living thereon prove my argument. You can see here in the audience about forty old men whose ages range between fifty and seventy that is, some of them lived during two consecutive foreign dominations; the Turkish colonization and the British mandate. None of those men had ever been to school! How many of them can read and write?. This proves my claim to be true! The Turks did not care about the education of the natives. They were just interested in collecting taxes. They left the Arabs illiterate. So when they were defeated. They left the Arab countries venerable to any invader. The literate elite, if any, were suffering from inferiority complex. They were ignorant, too. The Arabs were like the orphans at the banquets of the wicked ones. So you see the result now. The whole nation is fragmented and the countries are lost –the byproduct of the Ottoman Empire!

He continued: "The Ottoman Empire distorted Islam itself through building domes on tombs and sanctifying the dead. They encouraged people to worship and associate other deities to Allah. All the defects and shortcomings you see throughout the Arab world nowadays and for centuries to come are the bitter fruits of the Ottoman occupation! You can travel throughout the Middle East countries. I challenge you to locate a factory or any development projects that had been established by the colonizers whether Turks or Western imperialists. The sergeant commented that "the earth with its land marks or archeological sites and the artifacts therein make up for what the history books overlooked! Authenticity of history stories is certified by the reality that exists on the land. The most noteworthy archeological sites of the Ottoman Empire throughout the Arab world are the detention castles. They are as mushroom springing up everywhere. The building our force settling in now, has been one of these castles, come and see it."

Now, the sergeant said that he was only interested in solving the problem had come to settle. The headman said he had more to say, but   he would be pleased to see Hadjis and the goat- boy reconciled. Hadjis and the Shepherd were reconciled and the party was over! Muhajer, attended the meeting but a host of questions swarmed in his head: "Why were boys not allowed to sit down, laugh, or talk in the presence of old men? Why was the sergeant always right? Why did every one accept what he said without any objection? Why were the sergeant and the headman always right when they spoke? Why were children not allowed to dine with men?"

On their way home, the boy asked Hadjis those questions.

. Hadjis asked him to shut up, adding that the rules and the traditions of the community should be observed and its values should be respected: Never laugh, talk, or sit down in the hosting tent or room in the presence of old men. Moreover, you should give your place to those who are older than you are. You should respect the older persons. You should not call a man who got children by his sure name. You should use his nickname: Bu ….X. the name of first male child rather than the female child! Customs and rules of the society were not recorded. They were verbal doctrines, they were as powerful as the doctrines of religion. In fact, they had priority to the doctrines of religion. Men, young and old should always respect women, especially the women of others. A man should never slander any woman especially her honor! The honor of the whole village is pinned on the dignity of its women especially old women: young men and women should respect old women and obey them!

When Hadis came back to his cavern victorious after the reconciliation session, Rifqa was very excited and she received him with joy and happiness as a sign that she forgot his beating of her!

CHAPTER 2

Hadjis 's family had three guarding dogs. Himir Huqdi and Salwat . They were all husky. They were friendly to the family, but they would bark ferociously at strangers. Hadjis did not have to care much about the dogs, because they were able to fend for themselves. They lived on small wild animals like rabbits, hares besides carcasses. The dead animals would not be buried. They would be drawn out of the village and dropped in uninhabited area. Hadjis just provided his dogs with enough water. He put the water in large clay bowls in the shade of the trees. Birds would also drink from the bowls, too.

That night Hadjis and his family went early to bed, but at midnight, they heard the dogs barking wildly outside the cavern. Hadjis got up and hurried out holding his rifle! As he ran outside the cavern, the three dogs ran fast to the south where there was a wide opening in the grove's wall. They stopped when they reached the corner of the wall and seemed to put a moving object in the corner there. They were barking ferociously, and they began attacking something like a ghost. Hadjis walked towards them cautiously. When he was near enough, he heard someone moaning. He called out:" Who is there?" "O, my brother, help me!" a voice responded in the darkness. Hadjis went forward and asked, "Who are you? What's wrong with you?' the man answered that he was " Suweilim."

Sweilim , the outlaw. This man was wanted for the police for many complaints against him. Hadjis asked him not to move and he fired his rifle several times. A few minutes later, shots were fired from the hamlet, in response. The hamlet was horizontally about one mile away from the grove. There were many shots heard. Rifqa carried a small lantern and she with the boy and the girl went out of the cavern to see what was going on. She heard Hadjis shouting to the man " Move it ! Move it!'. She took a huge knob stick with her and went with the light in her other hand towards Hadjis . When she got there, she noticed that there was man with her husband. His calves were bleeding because the dogs had attacked him with their sharp fangs. When they arrived at the cavern Hadjis tied the thief with a rope to the trunk of the old carob tree after they bandaged his wounds with old rag shreds but they boiled water with salt and cleaned his wound. He began screaming when they poured the water with salt on his wounds. An hour later, some men of the hamlet arrived and told Hadjis that Dhughayyem his brother caught two thieves who were about to steal the two cows of Um Yunis , the oldest woman in the hamlet. Dhughayyem was a sharpshooter, he would shoot the bird while it was flying swiftly and he was accurate in hitting with bullets especially at night. He wounded the legs of both thieves with bullets. . The headman detained them in a deep cave in the hamlet. Hadjis told them that he had caught Sweilim , the famous outlaw. The men remained with Hadjis until the morning when they took Suweilim with them to join the other two thieves detained in the hamlet. The headman detained the thieves there until they were cured and could walk rather than handing them to the police.

All the inhabitants were proud of Hadjis and his brother Dhughayyem; they were the terror of the hamlet. No thief would venture to steel any animal at day or night; thieves were afraid of Dhughayyem in particular; he was famous of his accuracy in shooting!

Muhajer was proud of his father and he thought Hadjis to be insuperable. He would ward off any hazardous person who might attack the grove at day or at night. It was true that Hadjis was tough with all the members of his family but no intruder would venture hurting them. Hadjis would defend them against any hazards. He was their fortified castle that gave them full protection against external hazards.

At the same time, the boy was awed by Jabar's imposing character: he was for him a grand fortress that would protect him from predators, thieves, and hazards. Meanwhile Hadjis would terrify all the family members by his toughness and harsh treatment. Muhajer saw Hadjis break the head of the shepherd, kill the two wolves when they attacked the mule, and finally Hadjis caught an outlaw at midnight.

The dogs were dear to the boy, he would like to go to play with children of his age at the hamlet.. Himir would accompany him to the village; he felt secure when the dog accompanied him.

Peace overwhelmed that area for a long time. One morning, the weather was fine and the sun was shining permeating its warmth throughout the forest, A shepherd with his flock of sheep, was playing his flute at the plateau at the top of the mountain flanking the other side of the dale near the olive grove. His melodies were so tuneful that the birds were echoing them as the limbs of the trees gently moved with breezes blowing from the west, Hadjis, his wife and the boy knew who the shepherd was, and they enjoyed his tunes. Suddenly, there were shouts for help, the tunes of the flute died away giving room for the shouts for help: "Help! Help! Hyenas! The hyenas are attacking my sheep!" It was the shepherd who was calling for help. At once Hadjis took his Lee Martin rifle. He hurried to the stony wall   , the north wall of the border of the grove. When he got there, he leaned on the wall aiming his rifle to the north across the dale which was about two hundred meters wide and he began shooting towards the site of the flock. Two spotted grey hyenas were attacking the eastern flank of the flock, but when Hadjis fired his gun: the two hyenas fell to the ground growling with pain. The shepherd began dancing with joy and shouting "Stop it! Stop it! Bravo! Bravo! , you took both of them!'

Hadjis hurried to the plateau and found out that one of the hyenas was shot right in the middle of its head and it died at once, but the other one was hit into the rear left hind leg. It was gravely wounded that it fell to the ground but it was struggling to escape away. As the wound was very grave, it could not run away. But the hyena started biting everything it could bite; some limestones were crushed between its jaws. When Hadjis saw the hyena was suffering a great pain, he decided to shoot it in the head with what he called "The mercy bullet!"

The shepherd was very pleased with Hadjis   , this shepherd was as the same goat boy who had trespassed on the grove where Hadjis broke his skull .

Three men came on their horses cantering along the plateau. Seeing Hadjis with his rifle, the eldest of them shouted! "It is high time for you to stop provoking us! To this, the boy shouted loudly "No! No! Father! You should be grateful to him; he saved my life and the sheep. He killed the two hyenas attacking me! Look! Look!" When the old man saw the two hyenas lying on the ground, he felt sorry and went directly to Hadjis kissing his forefront and said: "I am indebted to you. You saved my son's life, you saved my sheep, and you deserve a reward." He called to his son and asked him to separate six of the fattest sheep and give them to Hadjis ! Who hesitated to accept the sheep, but the old man insisted: " Take them or I kill them; these sheep are yours.   Take them. Give their milk to your children and sell the lambs they will produce soon." Hadjis took the six sheep. He had to take care of those sheep daily!.

The goat boy told Hadjis that his father sold the goats because they liked to graze on the twigs of olives while the sheep would eat grass. Therefore, there was no harm of raising sheep instead of goats that caused many problems because they liked to eat the olive twigs as they were the worst enemy of the olive trees.

One day before noon the inhabitants heard the "azzam, the inviter" the coffee pounder sound echoing out of the hosting tent of the headman. Therefore, the men began arriving there. They saw the detained three thieves sitting in the tent and other three men with their Lee Martin rifles guarding them. There was a banquet held for the captives. After eating the food, the headman asked Dhughayyem and the men to compete in shooting targets.

The targets were small pieces of wood fixed two hundred meters away. All the competing men hit the targets. Hadjis availed himself well of this occasion to hit the bull-eyes of the targets. He was outstanding. He was able to hit a small needle dangling from a tree limb. He hit it directly though he could hardly see it. Hadjis and Dhughayyem hit cigarettes on a flat rock, they were both dexterous and sharp in hitting the targets.

Dhughayyem jokingly aimed his rife at the three captives who were terrified because the convention was "Men's outwardly joking is serious in depth" according to an Arabian adage.

The headman, released the captives after they had undertaken that they would never come back as thieves in that vicinity of . Dhughayyem commented that if he spotted any one of them in the vicinity, he would blow off his scull at once. He reminded them that they had shared food with natives of the hamlet! That meant that they should not breach their covenant not to transgress on the property of the people they shared food with.

The thieves were very awed when they saw how nimble and accurate the men were in hitting the targets. They begged the headman to keep the men in the hosting tent while the thieves were leaving the hamlet lest they shoot them then. The headman assured them that once they are given security that nobody would venture to break the tribal law that guaranteed 'the safety of the captives" when they were released and allowed to leave in peace!"

The three thieves hurried away and disappeared in the dense wood to the east of the hamlet. Since then, no thief had ever ventured into the hamlet or its vicinity as the thieves had learned the lesson well.

All the inhabitants of the hamlet, especially the children, were proud of Dhughayyem whom they deemed a proctor of the hamlet. Having the six ewes, Hadjis had to double his efforts not only to take care of the grove, but to ensure a good life for the six sheep that needed much water in that arid area, too. So he got rid of them quickly: he slaughtered two of them for banquets held especially for the forest rangers that often checked the area to spot charcoal-makers cutting trees for making charcoal!

The forest rangers would make surprise visits to the area and would stay as guests at the homes of the villagers , especially at the house of the headman who had a special guest house for the passers–by. Some of the forest rangers visited the place so many times so that they had become familiar not only with names of the main spots of the area , but they were well-acquainted   with the inhabitants, too. They knew even their habits of eating at the banquets. They knew who was gluttonous or greedy like Salbud, a miser who gluttonously feasted upon the banquets of the others: He had never held a banquet for any person.

The rangers, liked chicken most. Yet the meals, like the couscous, Maftool, were the most difficult ones for women to prepare. The ingredients consisted of wheat flour pellets. The host's wife had to prepare them manually. She would move her hand nimbly in circles at the bottom of a wide-open vessel to make the pellets out of wet wheat flour. Then women steam and boil the chicken with tomato and chickpeas!

The rangers liked the fatty old hens in particular. They would not be pleased if the host did not kill the oldest fatty hens in hennery. The   food had to be in abundance because almost all of the men in the village would be invited to have a meal at the host's house when people hear the sound of the coffee pounder – this tool was known to the villagers as the Azzam- the inviter. When the host crushed the coffee beans with this wooden or stone tool, the sound of coffee pounding and the rich coffee sweet-smelling aroma would be carried by the wind to the neighbors or the passers-by who would respond to that call and go the place where the sound emanated.

One day, the headman sent some young men to tell the inhabitants to meet at the hosting house. He sent them to the men who were living outside the hamlet like Hadjis and other men who were staying in the heath with their sheep and goats.

At the sunset the headman asked a young man to pound the coffee outside the hosting room so that all inhabitants hear the pounding sound-an invitation call for a meeting. When the majority of the elderly arrived at the hosting house, the headman asked them to sit on the mattresses spread under old terebinth tree. There, they were surprised to see Dheeb , their old friend who was a friend to all of them. Muhajer went with Hadjis and he was surprised to see a long scar that almost encircled   the old man's neck; the scar extended from the right vein to the left vein directly at the throat Muhajer gazed for a long time at the old man who seemed to be the oldest one among the men present. All the men present were happy to see that old man who was the headman of the nearby hamlet to the south of Wazeer hamlet. The boy was obsessed by the scar of the neck of the old man who noticed Muhjar's interest in him. Therefore, he reckoned to Muhajer to sit near him. The old man, cleared his throat and said:" Gentlemen, this boy has been looking at me since he arrived here. I know why! I think that the scar on my neck attracted his attention. Am I right, boy?"Muhajer timidly said: " yes." One of the young men asked: "How did you get that scar? Who tried to kill you?"

The old man sai: "The old men, here, perhaps remember the safar Barlik during the Ottoman reign of the Arab world. The Turks conscripted me and I was sent to Gallipoli front where the Turks waged a fierce battle against the Europeans. I was seventeen at the time. The commander ordered me to go with a patrol; behind the enemy lines where we were ambushed. We were seven personnel whereas the confronting forces were about 120. They encircled us and killed six of us, but I was not killed. The commander of the enemy took me to his tent and began interrogating me. I did not understand him nor did he understand me. So, he took his bayonet and tried to slay me. I tried to resist him but he was able to wound me from vein to vein. Old women, I think she was a doctor, took me to her tent and began treating me until I recovered. The woman was affectionate. She hired a boat and asked the boatman to land me at the Turkish coast. She gave me a small star to give it to the boatman by the end of voyage. She paid him half of the wages and the other half when he would go back to her after dropping me at the Turkish side. When we reached our destination, the man gave me some tinned bully beef and some Turkish money. I gave him the star the woman asked me to give to him at the end of the journey. The boatman had to show her the star to prove that he accomplished his task of dropping me at the Turkish side. It was early morning, I walked through dense forests heading south. The region he dropped me in was mountainous, so I had to walk haphazardly. I had neither a map nor a compass. I   spent two days walking through fearful forest swarming of wolves and hyenas. The old woman who had saved my life furnished me with a revolver and enough ammunition for it to protect myself in such a dangerous situation when passing through hazardous places. I used to hide at day and walk at night. One day, at dawn, I saw a lad who was taking two cows to the pasture. I hid behind a huge rock protruding at the side of a dusty road. He was about to pass the rock when I jumped before him saying:" I am in

Allah's protection and I seek your protection. "The boy was an Arab; he said": You are in safe hands. I will help you according to my capacity. He asked me to go with him to his father who would help me. He took me to his house but he hid me in the cowshed His father came to me. Hearing my story, the man said that he would help and take me to the border of Lebanon and there he would ask some of his friends to take me to Palestine. The next day the man brought two mules and asked me to mount one and he mounted the other. We set out on our journey to the northern border of Lebanon it took us three days to get there. We met some of the man's friends who took me in a caravan heading for Haifa. From Haifa I set out on my Journey on foot heading towards my hamlet. It took me two days to get there. When I arrived at the hamlet, I was shocked to know that my parents had passed away. Now .the story ended! The scars of my neck have lived with me so far.

It was a moon lit night at the end of November. Gusts of cold wind would blow from time to time. A cold gust blew shaking some cold leaves of the terebinth tree that fell to the ground, but a very cold leaf fell down on Salbud's neck. He thought it was a snake, so he hysterically shouted: "Go away. There is a snake on my neck". So the men were terrified and jumped to their feet at once, some of them tumbled over with the legs of others, falling down one after another and there was a clamor. Salbud , did not feel any pain , so he extended his arm and caught what thought to be a snake, he started giggling with his sah- sah. Saying:" it is a terebinth leaf! Calm down! "The men burst into laughing.

CHAPTER THREE

Hadjis's small family were staying in the cavern in their olive and almond grove situated at the highest peal peak , which was like a mound among the rugged hills ornamenting the lowest slopes of the mountains that flank the Jordan Valley from the west. It had a large extension of a very thick layer of rich soil; it was not strewn with boulders as the other areas around. In spring, the earth was covered with green flora, green shrubs and it was ornamented by rugs of new blossoms of wild flowers especially the white blossoms of ox-eye daisy. In January many narcissuses would bloom in the groves. The beauty of the area was intensified by the birds' singing in the olive groves while the breeze was negotiating the ears of the wild grass which were similar to the golden shiny wheatears. The west wind blowing would slant the wild oats to the east. They looked like moving shimmering water waves running one after another when the sun was shining and the sky was clear.

The child's mother, Rifqa, would weed and dig the ground beneath and around the olive trees. To remove the weeds growing in abundance after the rain season, she used an axe pick and sometimes a hoe to collect the wild weeds off the surface of the ground under the trees. She used a hoe to break the clotted soil under the trees where the earth was loose and the digging was easy, but she collected the roots by using the hoe. The weeds were taken off the loose layer of earth that was kept together by function of the intricate roots of the vegetation growing there. The grove's land was covered with gnarled and Roman aged olive trees growing sturdily there.

The trees of the grove were mixed: carob and almond trees which adorned the scene with booming immaculate white blossoms at the beginning of every February. But olive trees were the majority in the grove.

The females' life, wives and young girls was miserable. They lived under adverse conditions. The wife was an early bird: she would get up early before the sunrise to bake the bread either on a metal dome (sadj : bread tin) supported by stone trivet or she would bake bread in a taboon(an earthy oven); she would collect the wood for heating, cooking and baking. Some women would collect the dung of cows, sheep, and other animals for heating the earthy ovens. They had to do the laundry by hand; the homemaker had to take care of her family members' hygiene. The happiest housewife was usually the one who lived with her husband in isolation from the extended family; if she lived with an extended family; her life would be very miserable especially when she had a wicked old mother –in- law: The wicked old women sometimes would beat their daughters-in–law; some old women used especially-made pomegranate canes for beating their daughters-in-law. When the husband protested, his mother would beat him, too. Therefore, young women preferred to get married to a young man whose mother was dead. There were stories of justice pertaining to the treatment of mothers- in- law. One of those anecdotes was:

A young wife used to be kind to her mother-in-law. The the mother -in-law was living far away from her son's house. When the daughter -in -law cooked rice and meat, she would put some rice with a cutlet of meat on top of the rice in a tray. She would carry the tray on her head. Whenever she carried the tray of rice with the piece of meat on top, a falcon would plunge from the sky and snatch the piece of meat. This incident occurred many times .at last the daughter –in- law, told her mother-in–law the story of the falcon. The mother–in–law burst into tears and said: "I deserve it. It is Allah's Justice. When I was a young woman like you and my husband asked me to take food with some meat to his mother, I would throw away the pieces of meat so that she would not eat them. Now, God punishes me for my old sin of depriving her of eating meat."

Once Hadjis told Muhajer a story about God's justice pertaining to child-father relationship.. He said: "A young man got angry with his old father. He wanted to get rid of him. He started dragging him to a brink of a dry valley to throw him there. While he was dragging his father, the old man said"' that's enough! That's enough.!" The son was surprised. So he asked his old father: "how do you mean?" The old man answered "I had dragged my father to this point. So leave me here! I deserve it, but be sure that your son shall do the same thing to you!" Therefore, the Young man burst into tears and took his father back and he treated his old father kindly afterwards. So, Muhajer, be careful to treat me kindly when I become a very old man." Muhajer said he would do inshallah, God willing.

The grove was on the peak of highest hill in that area. From that height, one would see the best views: hills covered with sparse trees: Wild Lote(sidra) trees, green terebinth, pistaci khinjuk, pisticia lentiscus, Mediterranean mastic trees, and other thorny trees like Lote trees. The hills looked dark green but the continuity of the green extensions were spotted with large heaps of rocks and stones scattered everywhere. A legend says that when the Earth was created, an angle was carrying bags of stones and flying over the Earth and during his flight over that region the bags burst and the stones scattered all over the land , the impact of the heaviest rocks of them made troughs , dales and valleys throughout the surface of the Earth. The mounds and the hollows among the hills and the not arable lands were pastures for domestic animals and habitats for the wild ones.

In the early mornings of May , Muhajer would get up and go out the cavern and sit under the Carob tree enjoying the partridge callings coming from the opposite hill. He would also listen to dove cooing on the carob boughs and the nightingales singing. Throughout all the seasons of the year the scene was so appealing that it tempted people working in the groves and fields to stay working until darkness weighed down on the hills and the tracks that were difficult to see in darkness.

At the far end to the northeast of the hill of the grove, on a plateau settled the - Wazeer Hamlet; it was the hamlet where Hadjis 's family originated. All their ancestry and posterity had lived therein. During winters, the family would stay in the cavern, which went into the ground deeply in the grove. It was safer and warmer place and it was waterproof.

The house at the hamlet consisted of one large room with compartments, but it was door-less with a leaky ceiling consisting of dry branches and dry beams but covered with mud mixed with straw. During the rainy nights, it was impossible for the family to sleep because the water kept dripping on them from the ceiling. So they would move to the grove and stay in the cavern for the whole winter and spring. The cavern went underground: it had three compartments: The first compartment was for the family members it was large enough; its flat floor extended to the opening of the cavern. The second compartment was for storing the threshed hay, which was kept as fodder for the animals, and third compartment was for the animals: a donkey, a mule, and a cow!

Hadjis 's family consisted of two boys and a daughter, his wife and himself. The eldest son was staying with his grandmother (his father's mother) at Munqatta'a in Al- al- Aghwar (the Jordan valley). But the two children Muhajer who was in the last month of his sixth year and a daughter, Haleema who was in the beginning of her fifth year were with their parents at the cavern in the grove.

The inhabitants of the hamlet were posterity of a tribe living in the nearby region which consisted of several hamlets, the major village of those hamlets was located near profuse spring of water! As it was remote from the main cities, it was called Munqatta'a. It was one of 'the front line villages. The inhabitants of the Wazeer hamlet and Munqatta'a– belonged to the same tribe, settling in that area since the beginning of life in that region. They were divided into two clans; the first would take care of horses and cattle, so they were called the Fawaris, equestrians, and the other clan took care of sheep, goats and cattle, so they were called Kababeesh. Kabsh is the word for the sheep male or ram.

The UNRWA adopted Munqatta,a as a center for distributing the monthly aids to the refugees who were forced out of their homes during 1948 war. They settled in that area!

The UNRWA established a preparatory school there for the refugee's children and the children of the villages of the front line. Hadjis sent his elder son, Faruq, to the school there. The child lived with his grandmother (his father's mother).

Many of the Wazeer's inhabitants moved to Munqatta'a as the school was established there ; they wanted their children to go school, Hadjis lingered at the hamlet ; he stayed there to take care of his grove, the only productive piece of land he had in that area; it was at the top of the highest hill to the southwest of the hamlet: it had some old Roman gnarled olive trees ,carob and almond trees.

That place attracted Muhajer though it was muddy in winter. For him it was heaven, because he would entertain himself by the capturing scene of the land especially in February, March, and April. Winter and spring would adorn the uplands with multi-colored anemones, wild lilies. Spring usually ornamented the mountain slopes and the mounds with cyclamen, which were to the villagers sacred plants because they were associated to Mary, the Virgin. The little mound opposite to the grove hill was adorned with hyacinths flowers. The boy would pick up many flowers. By the end of April and the early May, a rich profound pleasant fragrance would permeate the whole region and the early breezes would carry the fragrance in the warm mornings.

The the hills were tinted with a variety of colors of flowers as the Creator have endowed them- each with one kind of flowers or herbs. Therefore, places were named after the flowers or the herbs growing therein. . One place which was a hallow extension of land was called Umm Khubeizeh , literary , the mother of the marshmallow. Another one was named the mother of tulips and crocuses!. Much of the area was wild and austere. To the villagers, winter was always the season of Allah's favors. The villagers cherished winter despite its very cold long nights

Winter was the season of tilling the land and sowing it with a variety of grains: wheat, barley, lentils, ervil(lentil vetch) and other grains. Not only did winter bring abundant rain to fill the villager's cisterns, but also it would bring forth different blessings: It was a season of healthy food herbs, too.

Some herbs were food supplies for the villagers like the marshmallow, which was abundant in many areas. Some families would cook the marshmallow daily, especially in the evening. When it was sunny and clear in the morning , the herbs would cooked on wood fire and the breakfast was served with yoghurt and green onion. People would sit on the grass and have the meal. The herbs were sources of food for both the villagers and their animals especially the cattle. Dandelion, chicory or fennel , gundelia and patience dock were other food herbs. Some herbs were medical herbs such as sage and wild thyme, which was also used a stable food for all the families in the morning. Mothers would dry the leaves and smash them into powder and keep the powder for the whole year in abundance. The thyme was the stable food for breakfast especially for schoolchildren, the powder was mixed with sesame, roasted wheat besides red sumac!

The sage would be added to tea, and it was boiled and given to children to treat cold or cramps. Mothers wouldboil thyme and give it to the ill children for treatment of cold. The life of the natives was peaceful; they knew nothing about the sophisticated societies and knew little of news of conflicts going on throughout the globe! Even they were not aware of the situation in Palestine itself. Nobody at that hamlet had a radio set!

At a rainy midnight in the end February in 1960, there was a stormy weather, there was a rapid west wind blowing, the villagers were all inside their homes, but some men were at the headman's hosting house. Suddenly they heard a very strange loud sounds _ a strange music and a woman singing! The men rose to their feet at once in panic. Some of them said: "A ghoul came to terrify the inhabitants" The headman asked them to calm down and told them what they heard was a song. He said that two days ago, Akuf went to Jerusalem and he asked him to buy a radio set for the hosting house. Therefore, the men began to laugh at one another describing how some of them were startled and worried, when they heard the sound.

In the morning Akuf brought the radio set to the hosting house. It was a tabletop Console style valve radio meant not be carried around. Families came to see the new device. They would would gather at the hosting house every night to listen the news from the London BBC Arabic Service. The headman encouraged the people to listen to that station because the Arab radios were biased and had prejudices against one another according to the political line they belonged to. The Arabic BBC Service, he said, was the most reliable and objective source of news. An old man, Bu Hameed, in the seventies of his age, said that he liked Great Britain news, because they were sincere in telling the truth. He lived under the Ottoman, The British and the Arab reigns. He could say that the fairest rule was that of the British. Muhajer noticed that the old man's lower jaw was twisted and broken. So he asked:" grandfather, what broke your jaw?" The old man was surprised to hear the question. He nervously said: "An accursed parent British soldier blew it off with a bullet while the British were chasing us in 1939!" The men burst into laughing. Hadjis commented: " This happened to you under the rule of the just British, what could have happened to you had they not been the fairest. Now I understand the meaning of the old Arab adage-"Be aware of the stories of an old man whose mates are dead!" Muhajer did not understand that Hadjis meant that the old man was a liar. He did not say the truth. When Hadis went home he kicked Muhajer hardly and cuffed his face several times for asking the old man that question.

There was no education in that region because hundreds of years had passed and not a single school was established there or throughout the Middle East. Ignorance weighed down on the whole region for centuries during the Turkish colonization of the Arab world! There were three generations alive in that hamlet: they were all illiterate: the grandparents, the parents, and the grandsons living among the inhabitants. Three consecutive generations without education, their ancestors were also not educated. Even Islam as a religion was not followed properly. People adopted practices irrelevant to Islam. They believed in astrology and augury.Most Women would resort to foretellers to sovle their problems. The dervishes were sacred; illiterate persons would build domes on their tombs and they believed in the divineness of such dervishes. This belief flourished during the dark ages of Ottoman Empire. Many of the practices like sanctifying tombs of holy persons had nothing to do with principles of Islam. The headman once told a story. He said:" During the Ottoman reign of the Arab World, two men were traveling through the desert on an old mule. When they reached at a juncture of a pilgrim road to Makkah, the mule died. So they panicked, but one of them was clever: he said to his companion: "why don't we convert our misfortune into blessing. Why don't we burry the mule and start weeping when travelers would pass by." They sat by the grave. After a while, a caravan passed by. So the two men burst into weeping, lamenting and beating their chests. The people of the caravan asked them why they were crying. They answered: "We have just buried our Imam Radji; he is a wally- a holy man. We want money for building a shrine with a dome on his grave." The people of the caravan donated much gold. Several caravans passed and donated gold. The two men collected a substantial amount of gold. Therefore, they decided to leave the place, but they wanted to divide the gold. One of them divided the gold into two halves and gave a half to his companion. The other man felt that his share was not as much as the share of his friend. So he protested and said the division was not fair. The other man said:" I swear by the sacred soul of our lord Radii." The other man said: "draw it a mild, you can't play tricks on me! Don't forget that we buried the mule to together. The headman continued: "the shrines of the so called saints sprang up like mushrooms during the Ottoman empire era. Superstitions prevailed over the minds of Muslims.

People under the reign of the Ottoman Empire used to steal the property of other families. Tribes would invade other tribes, take their property after slaughtering men, women, and children. Men would consider a peaceful man to be a coward that had never done something honorable- stealing or looting! They would pride on looting or robbery actions!

They would sit at night at the hosting houses bragging of their stealing advetures. An old man narrated that two slaves or black men went during a very dark night to steel some sheep of a Bedouin whose tent was at the outside of the encampment of his tribe. Reaching the tent, they sat behind the tent listening to a conversation between the owner of the tent and a guest: the thieves were able to hear the conversation clearly because only the long back screen of the tent was the barrier between both parties. The owner of the tent said: "I feel a very bad backache. The guest jokingly said: ' why don't you look for black women? Black women are good for treating backache!"

The two thieves heard the conversation. One of them said to the other: "This man is looking for a black women, we are black; we are her folks. So, let us take her dowry. The two men stole ten sheep and five lambs that night! They bragged that they stole the man's sheep because he thought of a black woman.

The villagers were illiterate and their ancestors and the fathers of their ancestors were too. This period of ignorance weighed down on the Levi and Mesopotamia for more than five centuries. Countries subsequent to the colonization were fragile. Any invader could easily conquer them! The Ottoman colonization of the Arab world erased all the civilization foundations as science and knowledge. It deeply dug foundations of ignorance that would last for many generations to come

There were other areas especially the slopes of the hills that were covered with dense forests. They were sources of trouble to the villagers who needed to cut down some the trees to make charcoal to sell to the nearby cities. Any villager or Mash-hardjy , charcoal maker, was caught by the forest rangers cutting trees down would be sued in the adjacent cities. There he would be jailed for a certain period if he were not able to buy the days of imprisonment. .The villagers there used to cherish winter because it brought with it the migratory birds like starlings, which temped the villagers to buy hunting rifles; they would often be pleased to compete with one another in hunting.

Hadjis was sent several times to court for cutting down trees, because the forest rangers would report him to the authorities concerned. Hadjis had a double barrel hunting zulu rifle and it was Italian- make which he was proud of

Hadjis was known as charcoal-maker. His face and hands were often black because of handling the charcoal, his face was light brown because of the effect of both the sun and the charcoal practice. The charcoal tinted it with blackness. His eyes would seem yellowish white. He was a heavy smoker of wild tobacco- or Hishee!

He was fined and sent to jail several times for infringing on the public forest areas. He obtained a permanent license, allowing him to make charcoal only from the trees he would cut down in his grove as it was necessary to get rid of the old trees that would be uprooted to create enough areas for the new generation of the olive trees he would plant therein.

Hadjis would cut down the old trees , collect the logs and cut the long branches and beams ,then he would arrange them in a stack that was arranged in rows around the important part which was called the chimney for the air to go though and he would make a few ventilations at the bottom of the stack !

He would bring burnt logs and throw them into the chimney   to heat the wood and evaporate its gases. That step followed covering the stack of wood with the falling leaves of the olive trees and cover the leaves with turf to prevent wind from going in. If it did, it would lead to burning the wood! After two nights, he would uncover the stack to find that all the wood had become charcoal .He would load a few donkeys or mules to transport the charcoal to the nearby cities to sell it there. The villagers would not use the charcoal at their homes. Instead, they would burn logs of wood directly to heat their homes in winter.

For Hadjis , winter was the best season to make charcoal, especially in January. He preferred that time because the forest rangers movement was limited due the cold weather and heavy rain.At night, he would wait on the charcoal so that it would not be burnt. While he was guarding charcoal stack, a fairy woman appeared to him at night. He said;

"It was late at night. I was sitting alone in the tent. Silence prevailed the whole place. Suddenly the two dogs that were with me burst in barking wildly. I realized that they saw a genie. When there was a genie. Dogs would bark when they saw a genie. It was very dark, but there was a small lantern hung at the middle beam of the tent. Suddenly, a girl appeared dancing in the middle of the tent. She had wide eyes sparking with red rays coming out of her eyes. She   would extend her hands and sing: "Take it is easy, man!. Life is easy! Do not care! Take it easy. It will be fine soon! Don't worry!"

She suddenly disappeared, but I was not afraid. I felt optimistic because she gave me glad tidings about the near future! The next day, a man from the nearby city came and bought all the charcoal I had. So she was a sign of good omen to me!

Though winter used to be heavy with long rainy nights, the villagers would cherish it and they would glorify their God for winter. It endowed them with riches of the earth: grass would grow for the animal as fodder. The region would   bloom with edible herbs like marsh mallows. Among the earliest favors of God was the wild mushrooms springing up near the huge rocks or under old trees after rain especially by the end of January and early February. The mushroom was in abundance; people would collect and cook the mushroom after rainy nights that witnessed much thunder. The villagers believed that thunder made the mushroom spring up in abundance! Those hills were full of mushroom in winter especially by the end of January and early February. Sitting around the fire kindled at night in a hosting room, the natives would tell anecdotes about mushroom. Muhajer with other children would often attend such meetings and listen attentively to the talks. One of the anecdotes was told by person whose name was Muserid he said:

One day I was plowing my piece of land at the upper part of the deer dale. Suddenly, it started to rain, so I had to stop plowing and go home. As I was riding my mule the rain intensified; it began pouring. It was impossible for me to continue my journey back to my home, because of the heavy rain. I was not able to find a shelter. Suddenly, I noticed something as huge as a gigantic umbrella .I hurried with the mule towards it. To my surprise, it was an enormous mushroom. God sent the jumbo mushroom to shelter me from the rain. It was like an enormous shade or umbrella! I hid with the mule under it until the rain was over. The giant mushroom was of great beauty .It was white with brown glistening patches: so I cut a great quantity of its round edge, put the mushroom in the mule's saddle bags and brought it home .

I distributed some of the mushroom to my neighbors. For sixty days, I would go and bring a lot of cutlets for my family and I would give the rest to all my neighbors who were forty families. .When asked about the place, he said it was near the vale by his piece of land. So , the vale was called the mushroom valley and the blatant lie has never been forgotten , it has been handed down generations and narrated as time passed by.

Villagers, of course, realized it was a blatant lie. Some of them remarked that he had seen a **rabbit** as huge as a big mule! The persons present burst into laughing, because if a person would tell a blatant lie, they would say it was a rabbit, i.e. a lie! Muhajer and a few children of his age would listen to such stories that were deeply rooted in their minds, but they enriched their imagination and sense of humor.

Some of the hills were covered with dense forests but other hills were covered with needle furze trees and thorny bushes of Poterium spinosum and other noxious weeds! Women did not like the furze trees growing there, because men, especially those who had wives, would cut the watery branches of the furze bushes, and use them as canes for beating their women with! But other more malicious men would cut sticks from trees of a hard branch of wood such the Palestinian buckthorn (Calycotome) which was very solid and it could stun the person or the donkey beaten with it. The sheep shepherds used to make plenty of them; they would carry many heavy sticks with them to use in clashes among themselves when they met at brooks or springs of water!

Women would take picks and axes and cut the needle furze trees growing near the hamlet or quarters of tent camps! They would cut down plenty of them to eliminate them from that area. Their pretext for cutting many of those trees was: to use them for cooking food and baking bread. But some wicked men would use other tools of punishment ; they would cut stout branches of trees to make clubs with heavy rounded heads, and they would beat their wives and daughters with. Women were treated harshly. the prevailing belief was that women should be disciplined by the stick only they are like slaves can be disciplined by stick.

An old man used to ask his elder son at night   if he had beaten his sister during the day. If the answer was no, the old man would order his son to wake her up and beat her though she was asleep! The villagers believed that women should be disciplined and should fear their males.

One evening Salbud came home with a heavy oak knob stick with a rounded knob. He was proud of it and he was swaying his body proudly. When he arrived home, he asked his poor wife if she had saved some meat for him. She answered that she cooked the whole meat for the children and they ate all the meat. Therefore, he was very angry that he lost his temper and hit the poor woman right into the head!

To his surprise, the hit did not hurt the woman. The knob of the stick was scattered into pieces all over the floor! The children burst into laughing when they saw the pieces of the knob scattered on the floor! Salbud said : "How come? What a flinty head you have! Believe me that I smashed a flint rock with it on my way home!" He had tried his knob stick by hitting a flint rock with it; it was his wife's luck that head of the club was already smashed as result of trying it

The harsh treatment of women did not mean that women were not dear to their parents, family, or clan. The society regarded women as symbols of honor of the whole clan. They were not allowed to marry strangers unless the strangers were proven to be of good reputation. The women themselves would feel ashamed if their husbands were not respectable by the society .An old; women once told an anecdote about a man who claimed that his clothes degraded his status among his fellow men: The old woman said:

Once upon a time, women used to pass by a hosting room; whenever she passed in front of the room, she would see her husband, Falih, sitting at the door near` a pile of shoes which were taken off there before the men entered the room. She would feel ashamed to see her husband sitting in that degrading place. One day, she asked him why he always sat in that place. He answered that he would sit in that place because the men did not respect him because the clothes he wore were not proper for him sit in a good place.

The next day, she went with her father to a city market where she sold her jewelry and bought her husband an Arabian cloak, white dishdasha, a muslin scarf , a golden reed head ring besides a new pair of shoes . She bought him a revolver with a red strap with glittering brass buttons.

When she got home, she asked Falih, her husband, to put on the new clothes and wear the scarf with his reed golden ring. She asked him to wear the revolver with its red strap!. She also urged him to go to the hosting room before other men arrived there.

Arriving the hosting room, he found no body there. Therefore, he sat in the middle of the row of mattresses spread by the wall of the room. Later, a man came and sat beside Falih . Another one came and sat between both of them. A third man came and squeezed himself between Falih and the man sitting by him so, Falih gave room to him and moved a little. Men would arrive one after another and Falih had to give room for every one of them by moving a little distance every time until he ended at his usual place. An hour later his wife passed by the place... She was shocked to see Falih sitting in the usual place. Therefore, she said nervously:" Shit is always shit even if his clothes are fit." The headman jumped up and ran to her. He asked her why she said those words. She told him the story of her husband and begged him to help her get rid of that rascal who brought shame on her. The headman was her uncle (her mother's brother). He was angry but pleased she asked to be divorced from him. He went home swiftly and fetched his sword, unsheathed it, and recited a verse in Arabic addressing Falih "Divorce her! You are not equal to her. Otherwise, this sword shall shatter the front of your head!" The woman went to her parents' house after the rascal was forced to divorce her!"

Despite their savage treatment of females, men had a great value for women. The honor of the man and his tribe is pinned on the woman. She should always be clean body and soul. The woman, to the villagers was a safeguarded jewel! If a woman had a bad reputation, people would despise her as a carcass that stray dogs feast upon!

As Hadjis was passing by the headman's black tent pitched at the foot of the mountain of the olive groves, he heard the sound of coffee pounding. He dropped by in response to the invitation. He said that he was looking for the rangers and he is pleased that they were there at the headman's home as guests. Then he whispered into the headman's ears that he would invite the rangers to dinner tomorrow. He begged the headman to accept a lamb he would kill for the tomorrow's meal! He said he had no place to receive the men and he liked that the banquet be held at the headman's hosting tent.

The headman welcomed the idea saying that the tent for all the inhabitants and he can hold a banquet at any time he wished. He promised Hadjis to announce the banquet soon after the guests would have eaten their meal!

Then the food was served in two huge trays with a heap of couscous pellets soaked with tomato soup and chickpeas; each heap was covered completely with cooked breasts and legs, backs of chicken. The leader of the rangers commented that the hens were fatty as an indication of his pleasure! The host asked the present people to help themselves! All the persons were pleased except two of them who were adjoining one another: Salbud and Jabbur; they hated each other because of gluttony backgrounds. They were known to eat ravenously without reservations or regarding the etiquette which entailed that an individual should not be the first one to start eating, because the first one who extended his hand for the food was regarded as the greediest person of the people there -an old Arab verse that was memorized by many people stated that:

'" When the hands are extended to food, I would not be the fastest to extend my hand to it, because the greediest among the people is the one who is the fastest to extend his hand to food!" the custom was the oldest person who would start first or the most notable one.

As the host asked his guests to start eating, Jabbur extended his hand first. It was like a nimble mouse jumping from one side to another to choose the best cutlets or parts of the cooked hens. His hand would pump against the hands of others who withdrew their hands allowing him to take the pieces he wanted. He would press the pieces with his fingers to see if they were fatty or boneless. Muhajar and other children were standing there watching the men devouring the food. In the middle of the tray at the top of the heap of pellets, was a fatty end (the knob of the tail feathers) of a hen back. It was nearer to Salbud , but his rival Jabbur , snatched it and devoured it at once, The leader of the rangers noticed Jabbur's action, so he   maliciously remarked " poor Salbud how did you let Jabbur take your share? What a fatty knob it was!"

Salbud was unable to speak. He had already stuffed the whole cavity of his mouth with huge rounded morsel of pressed pellets of couscous. He filled his right palm with the pellets , pressed them together making a heap of them filling the whole palm from the tips of his wide open fingers to the upper end of the palm ! And then he thrust them into the cavity of his mouth, some pellets were stuck at the corners of his mouth. He tried to gulp the extra-heaped morsel into his throat and at the same time, he tried to speak. He chocked and because of the pressure inside his throat, he was not able to control himself. Therefore, he began coughing. The commander of the rangers commented: "Gluttony kills more than the sword." Salbud ignored it, but the others started laughing.

Salbud leered his eyes at Jabbur and with difficulty tried to swallow the morsel. He started calling Jabbur   names, protesting that had devoured his portion without feeling ashamed of himself. Jabbur then said : " shut up your mouth which is like the mouth of a liar grey hound." All   persons whose mouths were stuffed with food burst into laughing, and a cloud of the pellets of the Maftool came out of their mouths and landed on the heap of the food! Most men refrained from eating, believing the food had become polluted. Salbud then struck Jabbur with a knob stick on the skull and blood gushed at once. There was a clamor among the crowd there. Then, the elderly pacified them. The headman said that the problem should be settled at once. Jabbur was very upset and he said that he was joking with Salbud and he did not think that he would lose his temper. The whole people of the hamlet knew that Jabbur was gluttonous, but he was generous. His wife would have the least number of chickens because Jabbur often had feasts for the visitors, passers-by and the rangers. So he was pleased to hold a reconciliatory banquet the next day. He promised Salbud that he would slay six fatty old hens that had fatty tail knobs and all the knobs would be for Sal bud . He would put them in a special tray for him. Salbud was intoxicated with happiness. The rangers' leader commented: "The one with a little mind can be pleased with chattering while the gluttonous one can be pleased with much food!"

Muhajer and a few boys were present and attentively noticed what was going on. They were waiting to eat.

A great quantity of food was left. Then at that banquet spoons were not used, because people were used to eating with three fingers of their right hand that should be cleaned before and after having Food, especially the types made of wheat bread deemed to be sacred blessings from God.

All People would pick up crusts of bread and kiss them and put them on their forefronts when they found them thrown on the ground. You would never see a crust of bread thrown on the ground. Some people would argue that it was cleaner to eat with spoons, but others said that the spoon would go into the mouth and then into the food, so it is the same in terms of pollution! . The accepted method was eating with the right hand rather, eating with three fingers to pick the food was a common practice. This method was adopted for eating foods consisting of rice and foods made of pellets or crushed wheat. When the men left the food in abundance Salbud and Jabbur were pleased and resumed eating that they almost devoured all the food with gluttony leaving almost nothing for the few small boys waiting for the men to finish eating , but those two seemed that they would never be satisfied!

Seeing that the food was almost devoured by Jabbur and Salbud , the headman who was the host, shouted to both of them saying " stop it, you have had enough food . You have devoured all the food, are you not shamed of yourselves.those children waiting to have their share of food. Why don't you be ashamed of yourselves?" To this, they reluctantly left the trays of the food and the children began eating the scanty quantity of the food left.

Men stayed after dinner listening a rebec tunes (rabab) played by Salbud! After a while the Arabian coffee was handed to each one present.

Suddenly, Muhajer came running towards Hadjis and said loudly;" Father ! father !I want to go to the gypsies!"

Hadjis was upset and got up chasing the boy out throwing some stones at him. The boy ran for his life and Hadjis came back and sat with the men . The boy continued running ,going back to the cavern in the grove where Rifqa was. He arrived gasping of tiredness; he told her that he wanted the donkey for his father with a cover on it. She gave him the donkey and he jumped over it and headed towards the hamlet. There he met a boy of his age, his cousin, Zeid, who told Muhajer that the gypsies sold traps for catching small birds. The two boys headed for the gypsies camp site beyond a hill about eight kilometers to the north of the hamlet. Zeid had gone there with Salbud to install a goldentooth. When they arrived there, Zeid told the gypsies that they wanted iron traps to catch birds with. Muhajer began crying: "I want my parents; I want my parents, my parents are here with you!"

An old gypsy woman heard him crying . She saw the two boys and came running to them; she asked the boys their names.She asked Muhajer:' who told you that your parents arehere with us?"Muhajer said: " Rifqa told me that you lost me in the heath and they food me there." The woman hugged Muhajer and kissed him crying: "My son! He is my son! at last I found you, Saffron ! " The Hibr of the gypsies , their chieftain , asked the woman what the matter was. She told him the boy was hers and she recognized him by a scar on his neck under his right ear. Zaid, ran away to the donkey jumped over it and rapidly headed for the hamlet leaving Muhajer at the gypsies' camp. He arrived by the sunset. He told his father the story. Salbud mounted the donkey and went to Hadjis 's cavern. When he got there, he found Rifqa with her face spotted with black bruises. She told him that Hadjis had beaten her heavily thinking that she had forced Muhajer to run away. Salbud was pleased to see her in that shape. He began laughing and asked her to hand him Hadjis's rifle. He shot three bullets in the air. An hour later, Hadjis arrived and Salbud told him that Muhajer was at the gypsies' camp! He told him that he went to buy a trap from them, but he told them that he was their son; an old women said that she was his mother. Hadjis got very angry when Salbud reminded him that Muhajer told him that he wanted to go the gypsies. Salbud was laughing indifferently, but Rifqa was terrified when she heard that the boy told the gypsies that he was their son!

Hadjis told Rifqa to kindle a big fire as she would stay the night alone with their daughter; he wanted to go and bring the boy back immediately. Then, Hadjis went with Salbud to the headman of the hamlet and told him the story of the boy. The headman was upset and he commented: "Why don't you treat your children kindly. The child left you to look for a better life; he

preferred livening with the gypsies to living with you. You know the folklore adage that says 'No dog runs away from a wedding party!' You cannot go now to the gypsies. They might slaughter you if you go there at night. Leave it to me I will settle the matter tomorrow morning as the adage says: 'attack your foes in the morning .not at night. In the morning is success. "

Hadjis went back to the cavern; he found Rifqa awake and told her that gypsies might not let the boy return home; they might take him forever. She started weeping, hearing the gypsies would not let the boy come back. She regretted that she once told him that he was a gypsy child!

In the morning Hadjis took his rifle with him and promised Rifqa he would not come back unless the boy was with him! The headman, Hadjis , Salbud and five other men , all were armed , went to the gypsies' camp. When they arrived, they told the chieftain (the Hibr) of the gypsies that they came to take the boy. The boy said that Rifqa once told him that he was a gypsy child and he was found in the heath! At last, he found his mother who had him sleep in her bed last night and she treated him kindly. Therefore, he would not go back with them.

The woman insisted that the boy was hers. She said that she recognized him by the scar on his neck beneath his right ear. The headman laughed and said; "Then I am your son. I have similar scar on my neck under my right ear. 'All of us are your children. We have the same scar under our right ears." Mothers used to treat mumps by cauterization. They would heat a metal rod and then burn the swelling part of the neck to treat the mumps."

The men burst into laughing and Hadjis said: "You have to give us the boy or you bear the consequences!"

The boy said loudly addressing Hadjis ; "I don't want to go back with you, I will stay here with my mother. You always beat me! She hugged me warmly when I slept in her bed last night , Rifqa never hugged me all my life. She told me that the gypsies lost me in the heat and you found me there. She hates me and you do,too. My name is not Muhajer, it is Saffron."

The old woman affected weeping as she listened to the boy. She got up and brought a trap, hugged the boy warmly. In addition, she gave him the trap. He was very pleased. He said: "you see! She gave me the trap without money. She is my mother!"

Then, the headman reckoned to the boy to go to him! The headman gently touched the hair of the boy's head and said: "My son you should go back to your parents; they love you. They treated you harshly, because they wanted you to become a man. I'll buy y,ou ten traps now and a rifle when you grow up. I'll ask Hadjis to treat you kindly!" He spoke up: "Hadjis never beat him and if you do, I'll be angry with you! " Hadjis nodded his head in agreement. The headman whispered in the ear of the boy:" This woman is not your mother! She wants money only. Now you will see. She will sell you!" then the headman said loudly to the woman: "Listen to me! We want our boy back. I give you two dinars for the night you took care of him!" The woman said I'll give him for five!'

The headman took five dinars out of his pocket and rose up, giving the woman the money! Then they took the boy with them and left for the hamlet. When the boy arrived at the cavern Rifqa shouted to him , "You came back , then, May Allah break your neck." But she noticed that swarms of fleas were creeping upon the boy's garments. She had him swiftly take his clothes off and she hurled them into the fire kindled in front of the cavern. Hadjis spoke to Rifqah and told her he would turn a new page: they would treat the child kindly and he would treat her kindly, too. He said he had learnt the lesson of what had happened. He said that they had to bear with the child, as it was their destiny!

An old woman came to headman's hosting tent wailing one day. She said that two ghost-like persons robbed her of the gold and jewelry she had. She could not recognize them because they masked their faces and it was too dark. She heard them both laughing upon leaving her house. She believed they were from the inhabitants of the hamlet.

The headman consulted the men around him. Deedis said that there was a Faqeer, an old scholar of religion living in a cave near Munqatta'a. He could locate the stolen things and find out the thief. He just uttered some spells to find out the thief. That Faqeer could do miracles ; he could make two mountains standing apart meet together,he said.

Convinced by Deedis, the headman sent for the sorcerer! The next day, the sorcerer arrived and he was received with respect .The headman with a few young men killed a sheep and invited the other men to come to have dinner on the honor of the sorcerer! The old woman slaughtered six fatty old hens of hers as her contribution to the banquet. She prepared Maftool, a matter that pleased Karandas , the sorcerer. The forest rangers attended the banquet which was held under an old oak tree with its shady branches. It was very tempting to lean on the wool mattresses arranged one by one with soft billows and cushions for the guests and the invited persons to sit on. The Faqeer asked the headman to fill a bowl with pure version olive oil from the house of the old woman. He told them that he needed an underage boy to look into the bowl of oil and spot the thief whose image would appear in the bowl! The only courageous boy was Muhajer who dared to sit by the sorcerer and look into the bowl!

The sorcerer started muttering his spells   concealing what he was saying and continued muttering for about fifteen minutes. He asked the boy every now and then:" Have you seen anything?" The   answer was no, but finally the sorcerer said with a strict threatening tone:" now the thief shall appear in the oil! You tell me his name" Then he muttered some spells and asked loudly:" Did you see anything, boy?" To this, Muhajer answered ; "Yes! Yes!" Then the sorcerer with a wave of happiness dancing on his face and his eyes glittering with joy:" what do you see? Tell us! Come on! "Then, the boy said nervously "I can see only the shadow of your turban!" People burst into laughing! The session ended in a complete failure but it ended with another catastrophe for the old woman who lost her   twelve hens for the sorcerer paid to him as wages, let alone the six ones slaughtered for the banquet, but   Karandas, the sorcerer,   promised that he would help her to identify the thieves.

Another incident took place. One night, an old woman came wailing to the headman's hosting tent; she said that her two cows were stolen last night. She accused Salbud and Bu Saleem of stealing them.

They both denied stealing the two cows. The headman asked them to swear on the Koran that they had not stolen the cows. They swore, but the old woman said: "They asked the thief to swear by Allah, he said 'Relief has come to me!' "She insisted that they were the culprits and she wanted them to go to El khader's Seat to swear there.

The next day Salbud mounted his mule and asked Saleem to ride behind him on the mule. The headman with a few men riding their horses went with them. They took the rugged dusty track descending to the Seat at the foot of the mountain near Munqatta'a ! Hadjis took Muhjajer with him to visit his grandmother and see his brother Faruq at MUnqata'a. Muhajer took a glass bottle with three hornets trapped in it. It was capped with metallic cap with some holes in it. As the temperature rose, the hornets moved violently inside the bottle . Muhajer was terrified and he dropped the bottle to a rock in the middle of the track . The bottle was   smashed into pieces and the hornets were set free. The dispersed rapidly.

It was a very hot day and the mule was waving its tail to cool itself. While the mule was doing this, a hornet of Muhajer's stung it. Therefore, the mule began lashing its hind legs wildly into the air, Salbud and Bu Saleem fell violently off the mule's back into the milled dusty road. A huge cloud of dust enveloped them, covering their eyelashes with dust.   Terrified, Salbud believed it was Sidi Khader who made the mule hurl them to the ground. So, he said loudly: "we are the thieves. We confess it." So the men went back to the hamlet and the headman asked Salbud and Saleem to compensate the old woman for her stolen cows. Salbud had no money and he promised to let the old woman his land as a mortgage for ten successive year. Saleem took his wife's jewelry and gave it to the old woman! Hadjis kissed Muhajer and gave him some candies, because it was his hornet that made Salbud confess his crime of robbing the old woman of her jewelry.

CHAPTER FOUR

One day Dhughayyem was sitting in the shade of an old carob tree. Muhajer who was itting there said: look there is a man ascending the steep hill east of the hamlet. When the man arrived, Dhughayyem was surprised to see his old friend 'Jaffal'. He had not seen him for years that he hardly recognized him. The man's attire reflected the wretchedness of the life he was leading. Dhughayyem felt pity on him when he told him that he and his family: sisters and brothers had nothing to eat except the dry seeds of edible thistle: They would roast them and eat them. Dhughayyem was very sorry for his friend. He promised him to solve his problem at once. They stayed the night together and before dawn they set out heading to the mountains to the south of hamlet. They came to a dense wood through which a paved road led to the center of the district there. At one o'clock in the afternoon, a bus was running along the road going to the city. Dhughayyem and Jaffal had rolled two huge boulders and centered them in the middle of the road. The bus stopped at that barricade. Dhughayyem appeared from behind a tree and swiftly ran to the window of the bus driver pointing his rifle to his head: he shouted to him to open the door and asked him to collect fifty dinars from the passengers. A man hurried out of the bus and went around the bus going to Dhughayyem saying some words. He came to him smiling and said: "Allah is glorified! a mountain never meets a mountain , but a man and another man meet even after a long time. My dear friend, you remember our watch word while were outlaws: it was Aba El-hitchew!" Dhughayyem left his rifle off the driver's head and said: "welcome Saad, my friend . Then, you are here to help us." He told him the story of his companion and that he needed money! Dhughayyem said he would not rob the passengers. He asked Saad to urge the passengers to donate money as charity to help the poor man with him!.

Saad went into the bus and addressed the passengers saying: "Dear brothers you know me and we are all from one village; we know each other well. I sacrifice my soul for your dignity. This man is my friend and I know him very well. His companion is needy. He had a wife and five children to feed. They have been living on the dry seeds of edible thistle for at least six months. He resorted to my my friend to help him. My friend had to to act like this. Therefore, I address your spirit of generosity to help this man. "

The passengers were moved to know how needy the man was. So they denoted whatever money they could. . The money was collected in a handkerchief; the boulders were removed and the bus resumed its journey. Dhughayyem counted the money ; it was 120 J.D. He gave his friend fifty and kept the rest for himself. So the venture ended happily, because of the generosity of the villagers who donated the money!

When Dhughayyem went back to the hamlet he had a big banquet for his friend. He killed two sheep and twelve old hens for making Maftool , the two sheep for making Mansaf for the guest and the Maftool for Jabbur , Salbud and the likes. Jaffal was very pleased with his friend Dhughayyem!.   The next day Dhughayyem rode his horse and went with his friend to his encampment. Dhughayyem told the story of his friend to Hadjis and how he managed to help him through the efforts of his friend Saad. Muhajer also heard the story while he was sitting there. He was very impressed by his uncle's action.

The next day, Hadjis took some loads of charcoal on the donkey and the mule to sell it in the nearby city. At noon, two men, wearing black garments and yellow scarves on their heads entered the grove.. They rapped their faces with scarves and went directly to Hadjis 's coal yard! They began packing the coal in some cases , but Rifqa hurried to them shouting: ' stop it , why are you stealing the char coal! One of the men wave his long stick and tried to hit her, but she ran away for the cavern. Muhajer was terrified; he ran into the cavern and with difficulty brought out Jabbar's rifle. He leaned it on a flat rock, pointing the rifle towards the haystack . Seeing his mother running away from the men, ,he with difficulty pulled the trigger of the rifle and fired shot towards the men. . As the boy   fired the shot, the men's mule fell down to the ground. It was killed at once; the bullet hit its head . The two men were terrified and they ran away. The jumped over the stone border and disappeared among the thick trees to the south of the grove. Rifqa emboldened by Muhajer's action hurried to the rifle and shot three bullets towards the trees the men disappeared among.   Hearing the shot, our horse equestrians came on their horses to Hadjis 's grove Rifqa told them the story. And told them that it was Muhajer that killed the mule of the thieves; they ran away, believing that a man was firing at them. She fired three bullets toward them. The equestrians hurried to the jungle the thieves hid in and searched it , but found no body there. Rifqa was pleased with boy . she gave him some candies and Turkish delight.

AT night Hadjis came back. Rifqa burst into tears and told Hadjis the story and how Muhajer terrified the thieves and by killing their mule. Hadjis was pleased with boy.

During those days, life was primitive. It was the life of the cave man in that area. There were no advanced technologies. People lived in isolation but peacefully though there were a few incidents that would disturb the tranquility of the hamlet. It was not a sophisticated society. Modern tools and utensils of for cooking were never used. People would use wood fire. They used wood logs and timber to burn for cooking. They used copper pots, dishes, and kettles for making coffee or tea. When the pots were used for a long time; their colors changed to black and they needed to be polished. So every summer, an artisan who used bleachers would come to the hamlet and stay under a terebinth tree. Families would bring their pots and kettles to him for polishing. The artisan used to dance while he was working on large wide-open vessels. He would add pieces of dry clay tiles and some bleachers. Then if the tray was wide enough to take in his feet that he moved dexterously as if he were dancing while he was   holding the trunk of the tree with both hands, . He would dance with a fez - tarboosh on his head.

When he danced the tassel attached to his tarboosh would sway rapidly in all directions; he looked funny especially to Salbud who would giggle loudly emitting a sound of sah- sah – sah! . Muhajer noticed the giggle of Salbud. So, he dubbed him as" Salbud- sah-sah."

In the summer of that year, one of the artisan came to the hamlet, and did the work for nearly all the families there except one family he refused to bleach their pots and dishes . It was Dhughayyem's family, Hadjis 's brother .It seemed that somebody, who wanted to make fun of artisan, told artisan that Dhughayyem would not pay him for his work! When Dhughayyem asked the artisan why he refused to bleach his coffee pots and other vessels of his family the artisan insisted on his refusal saying that he would never do the work for him. The artisan looked worried and tense. So, Dhughayyem suppressed his rage, keeping calm

When the Artisan finished the work in the afternoon, he mounted his mule and left the hamlet. Being away about three miles to the east of hamlet, the artisan was startled by the appearance of an armed man carrying along bamboo cane . He violently hit the artisan's right ear. Blood gushed at once. The artisan screamed. "I will polish them uncle. I will polish them uncle. I'll go back with you now to do the work for you."

Dhughayyem said, "No! But tell me who instigated you not to bleach the pots for me , or I'll bury you alive here!

The artisan hesitated to tell him, but finally under the pressure and the lashes of the bamboo stick, he uttered the name: "It was my friend , Sheloch, told me that you would bully me and would not pay for the work I would do for you!

Sheloch usually preferred to live in a secluded place . He did not like to socialize. He kept away from people lest he lose some of his wealth. He lived far away from populated areas. Even when he would take his sheep and goats to pasture he would choose a place rarely frequented by other shepherds.

He had many goats and preferred to live far away from the hamlet, but when he came across the artisan before the latter arrived at the hamlet, he instigated him against Dhughayyem and urged him not to polish the pots of Dhughayyem's family.

Dhughayyem   went home back in the evening and he asked his son Qassim . a lad of seventeen to go with Qadhi, Dhughayyem's nephew(his sister's son)   who was of the same age as Qassim's and asked them to roll a few boulders from the top of the mountain towards Sheloch's tent which was pitched at the mountain foot to the east of the hamlet. The two boys needed no spur, because they liked the idea of frightening that man and his family. There were many loose boulders at the slope of that mountain. They were smooth and rounded and they would roll swiftly as one would push them down the steep slope of the mountain!

When the two boys reached the point of rolling the stones, they looked for the heaviest smooth round rocks. They started pushing the heavy rocks towards the deep steep slope of the mountain. They counted: "one, two, three," and forcefully pushed the rocks which went down rolling rapidly and steadily towards the tent at the foot of the mountain. While the rocks were rolling down the slope they bumped against the tips of flint rocks protruding out of the ground. Bumping against the tips of the static rocks, the rolling stones generated loud cracklings like thunder rumbling. The slope was strewn with flinty rocks which emitted sparks when hit by the boulders. The area was covered with soft dry grass that was set ablaze. But the fire was not strong enough to overwhelm the whole area. It died away soon.

The rumbling of the stones awakened Sheloch, his family and the shepherds. The dogs started barking and four of them chased the two boys who fled hastily. Sheloch was a timid man who believed in fairy tales.. He was trembling and muttering that the ghosts sent the stones rolling towards his tent.

By saying so, he terrified his wife and the two shepherds' wives who were terrified to the last degree.

When Shiloh heard the stones rolling, he thought that supernatural beings were rolling stones   towards his tent, so he kindled a huge fire in front of his tent, using a huge quantity of dried bushy furze branches . . He began shouting at the top of his voice: " whoa! Whoa! Kish! Kish!"

The flames were blazing vehemently, at that moment there was an owl perching at the front robe of his tent. It was near the middle front wooden beam lifting the tent from the front. Sheloch saw the owl eyes gleaming in the blaze of the fire; he was terrified and thought it was one of the supernatural beings. The moment he thought it was an evil spirit. Dazzled by the blazes of the fire , the owl fell off the rope and violently struck Sheloch's chest! He fainted at once and fell to the ground. His wife began crying and all members of the family were terrified. A son of his brought some cold water and splashed it on his face. Then Sheloch recovered from coma, asking what happened.

When the two boys came back to Dhughayyem and reported to him what they did, he gave them a few candies and asked them to go to sleep.

In the morning Dhughayyem went to the headman of the hamlet and told him that Sheloch incited the artisan not   to bleach his pots. Dhughayyem asked the headman to hold Sheloch accountable for his unacceptable action!

A few hours later, Sheloch came riding a horse and the headman was pleased that he came. The headman asked Sheloch why he prompted the artisan not to work for Dhughayyem. He denied at first, but when the headman told him that he would send for the artisan to verify the matter. He added that would cost Sheloch at least four sheep to hold a banquet for the men who would attend the hearing session! Moreover, the artisan might demand a compensation for the time he lost in attending the session.

Sheloch was a miser man , as he saw that the presence of the artisan would cost him a fortune; he started laughing and he said: "Damn is his Satan !, Did he not polish Dhughayyem's family pots ? I was just kidding! But he took it seriously!"

To this the headman firmly said: ," You should reconcile with your cousin Dhughayyem. You should apologize for your childish felony   in a public reconciliatory session that would be held tomorrow at the hosting tent. You have to bring at least four fatty lambs for the banquet that will be held tomorrow! If you don't do this, Dhughayyem will never give up his right! He would not be pleased with you. In this case, he shall break your neck and it will only cost him a bullet from his rifle and he'll send you to hell!"

The next day, the session was held in the headman's huge black tent that was pitched in the shade of an old carob tree. At the beginning, the headman began his speech in the name of Allah and asked that Allah may bless his Messenger, Mohammad, peace be upon him, and he said that every man may make mistakes, but Allah would forgive those who repent their sins. Then he asked Allah's forgiveness, but the forgiveness will not be given unless the offended people forgive the offender, and in our present case. Sheloch offended his cousin, Dhughayyem, by inciting the artisan not to work for him . Today Sheloch is holding this banquet to apologize for his folly in front of you all: My judgment is that he should compensate Dhughayyem by giving him four sheep!(the sentence by the headman surprised Sheloch ,but he reluctantly accepted , affecting that he was delighted to give the four sheep to Dhughayyem.)

Sheloch stood up and walked towards Dhughayyem who also stood up and they both shook hands, Dhughayyem thanked the headman for his speech. He said that he would accept his decision and he accepted Sheloch's apology.He added that he would take the sheep and grant them to the old woman who lost her jewelry last week! The audience were moved and began shouting "Allahu Akber!   May Allah bless you Dhughayyem!"

Salbud was the most moved one; he took his rabab , played it and sang;

O, Salamah, when death calamities loom ,

I wish they roamed the rascals' homes one by one!

When silence weighed down, Halabi Abu Sha-ma , in his late forties who stuffed his belly with mutton and a heap of pieces of shredded bread soaked with mutton and tomato broth wanted to say something; he addressed the head man by saying :" Uncle Bu Hazeem, as he just uttered those words , he broke the wind loudly. The men burst into laughing. Muhajer and the other children present did not laugh fearing, if they did they would be rebuked by the men there. Halabi commented addressing his bottom end by saying: " Oh. I will not say anything! You talk! Accursed are the parents of your owner!." No sooner had he uttered those words than the headman slapped twice the back of Halabi's neck and shouted to him: "Get up! Get up! You don't realize that this place is not a place for farting, you should know that it is a dignified place for respected men! Go at once and slay a sheep for those men. We'll dine at your house in two hours!"

When supper was due, Jabbur and Salbud who liked the occasion   looked   restless. As they stood up, the headman asked where they were going.

:" To Abu Sha-ma's house! "They answered. The headman laughed and said: "What little minds you have! Aren't you ashamed of yourselves to eat the food of a banquet held for a fart! Sit down! Sit down! I asked the man to slay one sheep only and it is   hardly enough for his wife and children who taste the meat only once a year!"

Salbud and Jabbur were outraged but they suppressed their anger in their chests. Salbud addressed Jabbur:"You know, this man, Halabi, has never asked any person to drink a drop of water at his house, Damn may be the grey hair of his parents!' " Amen!" answered Jabbur

Muhajer , Zeid and other children witnessed the event and learnt that they should not behave indecently like Abu Sha-ma. Farting amongst people would bring shame on the person and all men of his tribe! Farting was a taboo! The animals will not do it!

The Rural life of the Palestinian villagers was the almost the same as that of the life of all Arabs of the Levi. It was a typical life   of peace and tranquility. It was the life of simple humble society. It was the life of a cooperative society, in fact. The people were peaceful and cooperative by nature.

Every community whether in a hamlet, a village or an encampment was presided by a headman who would allocate a special house or tent- *a* club for all members of the community. In villages and hamlets. The place was known as Medhafah or guesthouse. Every family used to have a medhafa. But the medhafah at the headman's house was the main guesthouse or club where strangers would be received and given free accommodation as guests. It was the place where problems of the inhabitants would be solved, too!

The Medhafah had a main sitting spacious room with lofty ventilations in the walls to let the smoke of fire go out, the fire would be kindled in a bit right in the center of the room. There Arabian coffee would be prepared .The fire would be kindled `in an open metal stove or in a hole dug in the middle of spacious floor of hosting room.

It was the dominant custom throughout rural areas of Palestine that the headman's Medhafah was the destination for all strangers passing by, or coming to the village. If the visitors were too many, the villagers would volunteer to help the headman's folk prepare enough food for them. Women would pull together at the house of the headman and help in preparing enough food

The inhabitants would go to the guesthouse when they heard the sound of the coffee pestle 'which is usually made of stout wood or metal to crush the roasted coffee beans in the guest house.' The tools and devices for making Arabian coffee were always available. There would be a bag made of deer leather for keeping spices like cardamom and saffron. The mahmas(roasting tray) for roasting coffee beans , the tray for cooling the hot beans (Mubarrid) ,   the keer- a hand low pressure air compressor   or Minfakkh for blowing air unto fire , and the melqat (fire tongs) to handle sparks of fire , coffee cups or (fanajeel) and the dallah (coffee pot).   There would be three dallahs(pots) at least. The coffee pots were made of copper; they were usually black because of much use on wood fire! The black pots indicated the superior hospitability of the host. The blacker it was, the more generous was the host.

The Rabab was always there.(a musical   instrument) During winter , the guest house was a warm club for the people of the village. At night fire would be kindled in the fireplace – a hole in the ground in the center of the main room. . Guests would sit around it after hearing the tunes of the coffee pestle .At cold nights, the men would wear long coats with fur lining made from sheep wool. There, they would sit, and talk about generosity to the passers-by, the visitors of the village, and the needy people. Those who were poor or they needed help to accomplish their work like tilling the land and they would have their problem solved by their fellow natives. Staying together at night during the long rainy nights, the villagers would enjoy eating the meals of maftool or musakhan roasted chicken with bread, they would eat mujadrah , boiled lentils with wheat or rice. Strangers who would pass by the village and had to stay the night or several nights there would stay as guests of the inhabitants of the village. They would have free accommodation because there were no hotels or motels there. Men of the village would take their sons to the Medhafah. Muhajer used to go with his father and he was so impressed by the stories and tales narrated there.. Some the tales were so funny and blatant lies that Muhajer and the children would not believe. One night, Bu Yunis , who would make up stories narrated:

"During the days of the British mandate of Palestine, people were not allowed to have weapons. But I managed to have a hunting rifle. One day I sneaked out of the village and went out to the deer's dale, you know it. When I got there I saw three gazelles. I at once shot one of them and hid my rifle in a thorny bushy tree. I hurried to the gazelle. When I got there, I saw another gazelle, so I swiftly aimed at and shot it at the spot. At this, Muhajer laughed and happily asked the man: " Grandfather, how did you shoot the second one while the rifle was in the bush?!'

Hadjis was angry and said to Muhajer :" Shut up boy! He went back to the bush and brought the rifle?" All the people sitting there burst into laughing. But Bu Yunis was embarrassed when someone said : " put it the saddle bag, " An indication of not believing the story. Another one asked Bu Yunis: " Are you sure it was a gazelle?. Perhaps it was a rabbit!" All the crowd there burst into laughing, because 'rabbit' indicated that the story was a blatant lie!

Muhajer was the first person who triggered the laughing of people there, but he did not know the consequences of it. Hadjis chased him out of the room and asked to go home alone in that very cold night! It was dangerous for such a child to go alone through a forest swarming with prey beasts. When the child was kicked out of the room, he found the family's three dogs , Salwat, Huqdy and Himir.

They wagged their tales for him. He was pleased to go with them back to the cavern. There were patches of white clouds in the sky and the moon would shine for a few minutes every now and then. When the boy and the three dogs were almost there at the cavern, the three dogs began barking wildly and running fast. They saw a porcupine moving in the southern part of grove. Therefore, Muhajer ran to the cavern and alerted Rifqa who came running to the dogs who caught the porcupine. She took it to the cavern and gave it water and kept it there waiting for Hadjis's arrival. Hadjis came at midnight! He was very pleased to see the porcupine, but he was not pleased with Muhajer , so he gave give him the bamboo cane and lashed him so many times, because he embarrassed Bu Yunis, the liar. The boy spent the rest of the night crying. But he learned a lesson "not to comment on the lies of older people!

In the morning Hadjis slaughtered the porcupine and Rifqa barbecued it on fire kindled outside the cavern. She kept the porcupine defensive quills to make a beautiful small tray of them!

A few days later, one of the women neighboring Sheloch came to the grove and sat with Rifqa. Mujhaer was there listening to their chatting. The woman told Rifqa how Sheloch was terrified by the owl that hit him directly in the chest when it was dazzled by the fire blaze. The two women began laughing but Muhjaer was listening attentively; he thought that he should be a friend to the owl that he saw every evening at the sunset at the carob tree near the cavern. He decided to be a friend of the owl. He had noticed that she killed a small lizard to eat it. So he decided to provide it with some meat!

When the woman left, Rifqa caught a fatty hen of hers. When Hadjis came in the afternoon, she asked him to kill the hen for supper. Hadjis killed the hen and he went inside the cavern to sleep there for a rest. Muhajer went to the carob tree. He saw the owl perching on the highest bough of the tree. He was pleased to see it there. When the owl sensed his presence, it started hooting : Tiwit tuhoo- twit tu-hoo."

Muhajar thought it was welcoming him. He was pleased and ran for the cavern. In the first compartment of the cavern Hadjis was fast asleep ,. Muhjaer looked for the killed hen. It was clean and cut into pieces and put on a tray on high rock in front the cavern. Rifqa used the rock as a worktable. So, Muhajer snatched a leg and ran towards the carob tree. Rifqa saw him and she ran after him holding a bamboo cane. When he got to the carob tree, he threw the leg to the owl that immediately dived and took it away and began helping itself to it. Rifqa arrived Muhjer gasping. She was tired of running up the slope leading to the carob tree. She held the bamboo cane and chased Muhajer who began running round the carob tree. Rifqa was shouting to him to stop, but the boy continued running round the tree! Because of the noise, the owl was startled, letting the chicken leg fall to the ground after it snatched some small pieces of it. While Muhajer was running round the carob tree, he saw the leg on the ground. He tried to pick it up, but he tumbled over though he got the leg in his hand. Rifqa started lashing the boy with the bamboo cane. To save himself the boy said loudly: "My mother! My mother! She is there, the gypsy, she is wearing a white dress!" So Rifqa was terrified and turned around, but she saw nothing. She resumed beating the child. He was screaming and holding out the leg of the chicken to Rifqa's face. The owl saw the piece of chicken near Rifqa's face, it dived violently and tried to snatch the piece of chicken, but its claws pierced Rifqa's face. The owl started scratching Rifqas cheeks and flapping her wings at Rifqa's eyes. Rifqa was terrified and ran for her life. Blood was flowing down her cheeks. She hurried to the cavern and awakened Hadjis who rose angrily. Knowing what happened from Rifqa , he hurried for his hunting rifle and ran quickly to the carob tree. There, he saw Muhajer crying , but he kicked him with his heavy boot and shot the owl. It fell <u>dead </u>to the ground. Muhajer was very grieved to see his friend, the owl, fell dead.

To avoid Rifqa's harsh treatment, Muhajer resorted to making up stories. Whenever she tried to hit him with the bamboo stick or something else, he would cry loudly saying: ' My mother! My mother! The gypsy. She is there. She is wearing white dress!" So Rifqa would stop beating him. In fact, she looked terrified and she mitigated her treatment of the boy.

The beginning of the rainy season, winter, would be known by the lightning flashes and thunder rumbling in remote skies beyond the clouds at night. the flash would light up the home gardens, the plains as if it were bringing glad tidings about winter! When thunder rumbled and rain fell, the farmer who had tilled his land and sown it with seeds of would-be-crops without watering would rejoice to see rain falling   to water his crops. Children of the villages would be happy in winter especially after rainy days. They would go to the plains and hills to gather the winter mushrooms that would spring up overnight. They would pick the wild anemone red flowers. They would be glad see herds of cattle going to   pastures. The life style of villagers was busy. There were many of hardships especially for women who were early birds : They would go to the forest early in the morning, they would cut   branches of trees and carry them in bundles on their heads ;   They would go in groups. Sometimes two or three women   would carry heavy bundles of wood on their heads. To protect their heads from being hurt by the branches they were carrying, women would put on their heads pieces of heavy cloth shaping them in thick round rings of canvass cloth. Sometimes, they would carry sacks of animal dung for their taboons .(earthy ovens).

The villagers were very proud of their homeland and region; their country was dearer to them than their souls or children's souls. They would leave their homes at dawn, especially the ploughmen who would take their animals like oxen, horses, and donkeys to till the land. While going to their fields in those hilly areas at dawn, they would see mad march hares jumping frantically out of the bushes and often they would see predatory beasts like jackals, hyenas, and the most hazardous, the wolves. To protect themselves from the wild beasts, some villagers would take rifles with them.

The dawn at the villages was the startup of the day. It used to be busy with movement. Life would wake up. The first creatures to wake up at dawn were the roosters. They would crow one after another. The roosters would crow at prayer times at dawn, at noon, in the afternoon at sunset and the late evening prayers. If a rooster crowed in area, another rooster would respond to him in another area! All roosters of the village would crow, especially at dawn and prayer times!

The second voice you would hear was the call for prayer if there was a mosque in the village, though the calling would not be heard in far quarters of the village. After dawn prayer, the whole village would become as busy as a beehive. You would hear cows lowing, sheep bleating, some people calling others loudly .All people who were above twelve years old would get up and set out for their fields or groves. Even children who could walk were taken to the farms with their families. Small children would help with simple things like collecting dry twigs for fire to make tea.

During winter when rain did not fall early, small children with teenage girls leading them would go through the dusty lanes of the village chanting rhymes of invoking God to send rain for the thirsty dry fields, farms and groves. They would chant songs of invoking God for rain. A prelude o song was:

> O, God our Sustainer
> We ask Thee rain of help
> To water our western crops
> We ask thee to water our sleeping crops
> Especially Bu Yusuf's crops
> For he is a generous man always.

In response to the children's invoking of God, house wives would throw some cold water towards the children, as a good omen that God would respond soon to their invoking. Two days later or often at the same night, rain would fall heavily .One night, no sooner the children had finished their invoking than it began pouring rain , the rain lasted for seven consecutive days.

The ceilings of houses consisted of beams of wood tree branches! They were covered with mud. So during heavy rain at night, water would leak through the ceilings of some houses; the dwellers would resort to their neighbors' houses who gladly receive them.

In an afternoon of a rainy day Dhughayyem's house was leaking. Therefore, when it stopped raining, he started taking his things to a neighbor's house. Muhajer with a few boys went to carry things with Dhughayyem.

When Dhughayyem was about to leave his house carrying a heavy mattress, his leg slipped on the dicey muddy step outside the door and he fell down with his heavy body. He was covered with mud. Muhajer was the first one to laugh. Then, all the boys there burst into laughing. So Dhughayyem shouted to them to stop laughing. He told Hadjis that Muhajer caused the children to laugh at him. So, Hadjis began kicking the boy with his foot. .

One year winter fell for two weeks and it   ceased to rain for about six weeks. Tith-tith , a man in the late forties of age , went checking the field of barley he planted two months ago; he found out the barley plants had not grown well. He lost hope that they would give him a plentiful produce.. Dhughayyem was sitting with a nephew, Fadhil , his sister's son, in his black tent pitched by a track going up a hill overlooking munqata'a. Qassim and Muhajer were there. .Tith-tith, dropped by.His face was pale and he looked worried! Fadhil asked him what the matter was. He said that he checked his field of barely and found that it was dry; he believed it would not grow well. He added that his effort would not be rewarded. Fadhil asked: "How much barely did you sow there?" Tith-tith answered:" One sack of 50 kg of barely." Fadhil; said : " I'll take care of the crop and I shall give you 50 kg of barley when I harvest the crop."

Tith- tith impulsively said: "by Allah and By my uncle's Dhughayyem's face I accept your offer.' If you get any barley , don't give it to me , give my share to this child; I offer it to him in advance.

The two parties agreed, but Dhughayyem guaranteed that Tith-tith would fulfill his promise. Fadhil mounted his mule and went to the land where the barely crop was. There was a plentiful brook of water flowing in a gutter by the piece of land of the crop. He started digging a hole in the gutter and diverted the water towards the barely crop. The water flooded the field for three consecutive days. It thoroughly soaked the field. Then Fadhil closed the opening and went home. Two weeks later he checked the field and found out that the barely had grown fast and it was flourishing well. He was pleased.

In summer. Fadhil harvested the field of barley and got a quantity of barely, about six hundred k.g. Thit-tith was not pleased and he said that he would take all the barely because it was his own field. Fadhil said:

I toiled all the year to get this produce . I exerted my best efforts grow the crop . I weed it, harvested and threshed it "You   have to abide by   the   deal guaranteed by uncle Dhughayyem." They both went to Dhughayyem and asked him to settle the problem. Dhughayyem intelligently said :" look , men are bound to their words ; they are not donkeys tied with a rope and a wedge in the ground. You should remember that you accepted me to guarantee the deal, Tith-tith! you involved my face in the deal and Fadhil agreed . This entailed that you accepted my settlement. Both of you have toiled to produce the barely and you involved me in the process. So every party must have his own share. So the parties involved are three. You ,Fadhil, got six hundred kilograms , the product. Therefore, the six-hindered kilograms shall be divided by three. i.e. 200 kg for every party. Agreed? 'The two conflicting parties agreed and thus, the conflict was settled Dhughayyem's sagacity.

Fadhil reminded Tith-tith of his promise to give his share to Muhajer. Tith–tith was embarrassed; he had to fulfill his promise. He said he would give Muhajer some money instead. He gave two dinars to Dhughayyem who kept them for Muhajer.

Living in a cooperative society, women would help each other repair the ceilings of houses and sometimes they would co-operate to dye the walls of their houses with white lime! Maintenance of the houses , blowing the fields in winter and harvesting the crops in summer were all collective activities , no one should be left alone; those who would finish their work earlier than their neighbors, would rally and go helping the other farmers who had not finished plowing their fields or harvesting their crops.

At the sunset of the evening of a day at the beginning of May, the coffee pounding sounded out of the hosting room of the headman of the Wazeer Hamlet. The pounding sound meant that there would be a meeting that night to discuss important matters. After most men had supper at their homes, they began arriving one after another at the hosting house. When the majority of men arrived, they had coffee as usual.

The headman told the present men that the harvest season would commence soon. He reminded them that the harvest season was the time of solidarity and cooperation among the inhabitants and he urged them to help the persons who needed help. He mentioned some names of the people who were in need of help, because they were too old to carry the work out by themselves. He mentioned to them as an example "Um Ahmad" , an old woman who was taking care of her fatherless little grandchildren. She had no body to do the work for her!

Two young brothers responded at once. One of them said: "My brother and I will do the work for her. There is an adage that says that 'The one who does a favor should do it wholly.' As you know, we had tilled and sowed her land in winter. Therefore, we will harvest the crops for her! We will also take it to the stack yard and thresh it for her. We will do all the required work for her!" The headman was very pleased with the two brothers.

Other young men said that they were ready to help anybody who needed help in gathering their crops; they would pass by all the crop fields and if they spot a person who needed help, they would help him. The headman and other old men were pleased with the young men. They said:" we are proud of your generation! This is the true spirit of our cooperative society, we will live in prosperity as long as this spirit dominates our customs and traditions. Keep it up."

The end of May was the beginning of the harvest season in the hilly areas; the villagers would harvest their crops of wheat, barley, and other crops.

Prior to the harvest, farmers would go and check their fields to make sure that the crops were ripe enough to harvest!

The headman, Abu Hazeem, had large wheat crop in a located between two hills to the south of the hamlet. That area was an abode for sheep and goat keepers who would stay for the winter in that area adjoining the wheat crop, but they would take care that their animals would not come near the crop!

The next day, Abu Hazeem, the head man of the hamlet , went to check his crop. When he got there, one of the men living there, invited him to take a rest at his tent;Abu Hazeem agreed. When he arrived there more men came and they began chatting. One of them said:" Abu Hazeem, we noticed last night that the cave at the peak of the opposite hill was lit up and the light lasted for a few minutes! The event had occurred by the end of every month for the last six months successively."

To this Abu Hazeem affected some awe on his face and looked as if he were shocked. He said: "In the name of Allah! "Have you sacrificed some of year sheep or goats whenever you saw it?" The answer was "No!" SO, he affected more fear and astonishment and muttered: "Forgive them my Lord, Kondreish! My Lord Kondreish ! They are simple and they don't know that it was Your Presence that haunted that cave monthly!" He cleared his throat and said: "listen men! You do not know that the light you saw was the light of the Lord of this area, Shake Kondreish, the offspring annihilator, who lived in this cave two hundred years ago! This cave was his abode. That man was a Faqeer , he would walk on the surface of water and through his blessings he endowed children to barren women , he did wonders! Don't you see that you, your children, your wives, and even your animals sometimes tumbled over while walking?" The men were surprised and nodded their heads! He added:"Your chieftain must hold a big banquet. You should kill at least seven of your goats or sheep whenever you see the light! Otherwise Sidi , My lord and yours ‚Kondreish , will not be pleased with you! He will annihilate your offspring and your animals if he is not pleased with you!"

One of the men asked:" If he had been able to do miracles, why did he live in that miserable place, in a cave like that?"

Abu Hazeem did not expect such a question. He thought for a moment and said:" You know everything in this life consists of two dimensions: the physical one and the spiritual one. The part that you can see, touch or taste. The abstract one that you cannot see or touch like your spirit. The body is the physical prison for the soul. It traps your soul and enslaves it. Those superb pious people are the ones who are able to escape the prison and live freely. They can live happily wherever they are free of the body constrains even if they have to live in a snake's hole. Physical things are the root cause of life's miseries. When they are simpler, life becomes easier. Our lord Kondreish would have lived in misery if he had lived in the most luxurious palace , his soul did not enjoy physical life in a more sophisticated palace. Of course, he is free in the cave. Therefore,   this cave for Sidi Kondreish was more enjoyable than the life in a luxurious palace. At the cave he lived more freely, there were no creatures to watch him. He lived more comfortably there than living in a palace where he would be subject to the constrains of the physical entities. He would be subject to the rules there. Do you know those who live in such places are not free like those who live alone in a cave. The master of the palace cannot live freely. His servants confine his actions. He cannot act freely in the presence of his subjects. Kondreish and persons like him are the people of Allah. They find satisfaction in everything that God endowed to them .contentment for them is ultimate end they aspire to. The watchword for them is contentment is the most important thing in life! Their motto is:

He continued: You don't know that Kondreish   is renown by the name " Shake Kondreish Qatta'a (annihilator) el-therary(posterity or offspring) ; you will lose your children if you do not honor His Presence!"

Two men rose up and hastily slaughtered two fatty sheep and cut one of them into culets, wrapped the meat with pieces of cloth and offered it to Abu Hazeem who wanted to leave the place. He said: "A place where Sidi Kondreish is not honored, I should not stay in for a long time ! Let me leave, I have no time for dinner!   . Today this sojourn will cost me at least four sheep to be slaughtered to have a banquet for the people of the hamlet. I am sure he saw me, if I don't honor him, he may break my neck!"

Thus, Abu Hazeem won one of the sheep and invited his friends to feast upon it.   It was a fatty meat with couscous. He surprised Jabbur , his brother and Salbud who were above the moon when he invited them. It was a surprise for both of them; he told them the story of Kondreish and the shepherds!

By, the end of every month the head man would force some teen agers were to go under the cover of darkness and kindle a fire in that cave! So, the next day Abu Hazeem would appear there, he would be present at the banquets held by the shepherds on the honor of Sidi Kondreish. ! The event was repeated a number of times. One night, one of the boys who was forced to go the cave and who would be afraid of walking in the darkness, decided to let the cat out of the bag! As the boys reached the cave,   they kindled the fire. ,The angry boy who decided to thwart Abu Hazeem's plan , shouted loudly " You idiots , we are Abu Hazeem's boys and he sends us to kindle fire in this cave so that you kill your sheep , don't you see that he appears in this place in the morning following the night the fire is kindled at the cave . Don't believe him! Kondreish is a hoax."

So the shepherds were perplexed; some believed the caller, but the women did not believe what they heard. One of the women, who became pregnant after slaughtering three lambs for Kondreih, did not believe that call. She said that it was the Satan who was calling.

The next morning, Abu Hazeem arrived   and he was told the story of the voice they heard. Abu Hazeem said to them :" You are poor! You do not know the reality; the voice you heard was not the voice of a real man. It was the voice of the devil .you should know that every Sufi Faqeer has a devil enemy! That was his enemy who wanted to trigger hostility and hatred among you, between you and me. Be assured that I am above such childish tricks. If I wanted some sheep from you, I would ask for them directly and you would not refuse my request!" The men were pleased to know it was the devil's sound, so they decided to leave that place and never live in that place forever!. They realized that it was Bu Hazzem , not Kondreih , who would annihilate their sheep !

Thus, Abu Hazeem was able to hit two birds with one stone; he got rid of the shepherds that were hazardous to his crops but he gained some of their sheep

CHAPTER FIVE

The harvest season, like winter, was a manifestation of cooperative peaceful life! Tilling the land was the hardest stage. Those seasons would reflect a bright image of the solidarity of the society: No one who needed help was disregarded by his brothers, neighbors, acquaintances and the society around him. The villagers would pull together to help each other finish the work in time. If someone of them were not able to till his land in time, his friends would bring their oxen and members of families to sow the seeds and till the land. With their help, the farmer would ensure that his land had been sowed and tilled properly before the rainfall.

During summer, you would see teams of twelve or sometimes twenty young men going in the early morning to help one of the natives of the village! Nobody was neglected .In return, if the farmer was well-off, he would provide food and water for the volunteers. If he were not able to offer food, his neighbors would do that for him.

Often children of the poor families, women and girls would search the harvested field looking for falling wheat ears. Those people were allowed to enter any field as they were known as wheat ear pickers or collectors! ; They would collect them in bouquets. Generous farmers would feel pity on those poor people. So they would offer them some wheat. It was a sure custom to leave some of the wheat not harvested for the poor to collect. If a farmer did not leave some of his crops for the poor, it would be stigma for him-he would be known as a miser!

The helping process would continue when the harvest was taken to the area usually located in the eastern part of the village where the crops would be transported on the back of camels, mule's, donkeys and wagons drawn by horses. Life was very peaceful. Nobody would transgress on others, they had their values and customs respected and observed. The young would respect the elderly men or women. When a young man would meet a woman regardless of her age, he would give her the right of way especially when they would meet in a dusty narrow track! In the meeting places or homes, the best seats were offered to the elderly, with respect. No young man would speak louder than the speech of his father. Coffee would be served from right to left or offered to the elder person there. If the father of the young man serving the offer was present, he would offer the coffee cup to his father first

The harvested crops were stacked at the area of stacks, usually at the east of the village, because west wind in summer was the most frequent wind that blew at night. Therefore, stacks of hay were accumulated in the eastern yard to the keep the houses clean of the threshed hay the wind would carry with it. . The crops would be transported on camels, horses. Mules and donkeys. The stacks would remain there for eight weeks at least. This place would be like a bee hive, or an ant village! You would see almost all the inhabitants there, especially in the afternoons. Young women would go in groups of three, or four to the stacks to collect earless stalks of wheat for making straw trays. They would soak the stalks in water and would dye the stalks with, black, red , green ad yellow colors . They would make flat round trays of straw with the star of the country's flag (the Flag of the Hashemite Kingdome of Jordan) in the middle of the tray. The straw trays were ornamented with rows of different colors. Moreover, they would make bowls for measuring flour. (quba'a) besides making large straw bowls for preserving bread .some girls would collect leafless stalks of wheat but with ears intact on them and make bouquets and hang them on the whitewalls of their rooms .

During moonlit nights the threshing at the stacks would go on! The person who would stand on the heavy wooden board strewn with stones of basalt would let the horse drag the threshing board around the stack until the stalks become powder. Then, a new quantity of stalks would be spread around the haystack and threshed. This process would last until the whole stack was completely threshed.

The working man, standing or sitting on the board, would sometimes sing loudly, especially when he would see beautiful girls passing by or coming to the stack. The prelude of a famous song was:

How often had I warned you,
The gazelle of the wilderness
Against taking the northern track;
The Turkmen might hunt you and
Make a rabab of your skin

Muhajer used to go to one of his uncle's stacks and sit on the threshing board for hours. The horses would go round while he was sitting with his uncle on the threshing board drawn around the stack by the horse.

The beautiful unmarried young women would go to the stack area. Many of them would attract the attention of bachelors or men who were looking for wives; the season was a harvest season that would create new families. It was impossible for young men and women to talk or meet openly nor privately. If a young man wanted to know that one of the girls was willing to marry him, he would know through smiles, and he would send his mother or sister to go and ask the girl if she agreed to marry the young man. The marriage would be settled through contacts of the women of the two families, especially the two mothers. But sometimes, the efforts would be thwarted if a wicked malice old grandmother of the man or the girl would intervene. She would instigate the cousins of the girl to ask for her hand in marriage to thwart the girl is marrying a stranger! The parents would prefer getting their daughters married to their nephews or kinship men. When the mother, aunts of the suiter would go to see the girl he wanted to army, they would take with them a nut, a needle and thread. His mother would sit by the girl and ask her to break the nut with her teeth, to ensure that her teeth were good.. if she broke the nut she would ask her to insert the string through the needle eye to make sure that her vision was good and the mother would also smell her by sitting closely to her to ensure that she had no bad B.O.(body odor)

In some cases , when the suitor resorted to influential persons in the village who would press the girl's father and persuade him into agreeing to his daughter's marriage to a stranger, the parents of the stranger would say that they fractioned an onion in her cousin's eye thy broke his nose. This would mean humiliation not only for her family but also for the entire clan. Male cousins, the father's brother sons, would have priority to marry their female cousins.

In some cases when the two parties would fall in love, but the family of the girl was too stubborn to allow the marriage, the girl would kill herself by burning either herself or throwing herself in a deep old ruin cistern. In this case, the suitor would not be left in peace; he would be accused of tarnishing the honor of the family of the girl and her clan. A few days or a week would pass when the suitor would be found killed or badly injured because of vengeance reasons!

The rural folklore of Palestine reflected the peaceful life of the Palestinian people This did not mean that there were not any individual disputes and clashes among people.. Such problems were easily overcome. By observing the spiritual and materialistic folklore handed down generations, it was a folklore representing various aspects of life that were summed up in one word :peace! That folklore was abundant of creative practices like folk poetry, songs expressing different moods of life with its joyful and sorrowful events. It reflected the styles of life types of wedding celebrations, circumcisions of boys, festivals. They would preserve the identity and the unity of the people who originated in that land from the beginning of life!

What characterized the villager's life during the harvest season were the light songs:

Noticing that a villager was not able to harvest his crops in time his neighbors pulled together to help him and they began singing in unison:

A crop I harvested while soaked with dewdrops for
Bu Hazeem by Allah's name to preserve him
The crops I harvested from the edge of the dale
The owner of which is a knight!

One summer, some friends pulled together to collect the harvest for Hadjis in rented piece of land . Mahajer had a role in the harvest by providing the men helping his father with water and food prepared by Rifqa. She would send the food and water loading them on the donkey .Muhajer would ride the donkey taking the supply of the food to the men who were doing the work at his father's field that he hired from an old woman who was not able to till the land by herself. The men were very pleased with him and they would say to him ' bravo."

While Muhajer was riding a donkey, heading for his father's field to send the food for the people working there. , a man was running his horse fast. Muhajer was not able to swerve the donkey from the road. Seeing the horse rushing towards him, Muhajer waved along stick as the horse approached him. The horse was startled, throwing the rider violently unto the dusty track. Dust covered the man .who got angry with Muhajer. He took Muhajer off the donkey's back and threw him to the ground! The boy burst into crying, but a young man, Fadhil , Muhajer's cousin , his aunt son, a shepherd with his sheep by the foot of the mountain, saw what happened. He shouted to the man::"why did you throw the boy to the ground?" The man who was named Bu Khalid of the Kbabeesh clan, said : ' he fell off the donkey by himself.' Fadhil said ;" I saw you throw the child off the donkey to the ground. You tell lies!" Bu khalid, seeing the man's size was little, angrily and   arrogantly said:" to hell with you , you son of abitch!"

To this, Fadhil struck the man with the knob stick on his head. The man fell to the ground and Fadhil restlessly rained him with beats with the knob stick.! Muhajer rode the donkey and resumed his journey towards his father's field. He told his father what happened. Hadjis was pleased with his nephew , the son of his sister. He held a great banquet for him and invited many people to it, among them was Bu khalid , who apologized for his felony and begged Hadjis to reconcile him with Fadhil who accepted his apology.

In May Sheloch collected his harvest of sesame. He filled eight sacks of sesame. Each sack had 50 K.G. Muhajer , went with Zeid, his cousin to the stack yard where Sheloch's produce was. Seeing the two children playing there, he filled two small bags with sesame; each bag containing about 2. Kg. he gave them to the two boys as presents for their families . The two boys were pleased and went home carrying the bags. When they were about two hundred meters away, he mounted his horse and ran after the boys. He was shouting loudly. When he reached them, he started hitting them with his bamboo cane. The two boys began screamming; they threw the two bags to the ground and fled into two directions one to the north and the other to the south .so he failed to hit any of them. The two boys continued screaming loudly. A shepherd who was grazing his sheep there heard and saw what was going on. Therefore he unleashed his two huge dogs against Shelock's horse. The two dogs burst into wild barking. The horse was startled and the two dogs began chasing the horse that ran fast. Terrified by the dogs, the horse jumped over a huge rock and violently threw Shelock down to the rugged road. He began screaming. Some men hurried to him and helped him to walk and they sat in the shade of a carob tree. He was badly injured. When asked   what the matter was, he accused the two children of stealing the two bags. The boys came back to the men when they summoned them. They said that Shelock gave them the two bags. Dhughayyem arrived at the scene , but he got very angry to see his nephews humiliated by Sheloch. He examined the two bags and noticed that they were sewn with a needle firmly that no grain of sesame would fall out of the bags. He addressed Shelock :"Look! You are a liar, can you explain to me how the two bags were sewn with pieces thread and a needle? Those two children, cannot seal the two bags with a needl. do this. " Moreover , the two boys said that he agve them the bags and asked them to take them home for their familis as presents.

Dhughayyem smiled maliciousely and looked at Sheloch sayng : " Bear the consequneces.!"

It was late after midde night, when Dhughayyem,Jabbur ,salbud and Hadjis took four mules and set out for Sheloch's sesame stack yard. There they foud him sleeping. Beside him were eight sacks-fifty k.g each, ready for tarnsporting. They loaded every two sacks on a mule. Sheloch noticed them. He recognized them, but pretended that he was fast a sleep! .

Dhughayyem struck him with the butt of his rifle . Shelock jumped to his feet' Dhughayyem said to him: " Listen Sheloch. I swear by Allah. If you mention this to any body , I shall blow off your head. You had incited the artisan against me but I forgave you . then, you accused our children of stealing sesame from you. You should know that if we wanted anything from you , we we would take it by force. Now you see and hear me! I warn you for the last time : Never provoke me or any one of my family . even it is a child. Next time, we shall not take any thing from you , but I assure you that it would be the end of your life. "

In the morning Dhughayyem went to the head man and told him the story of Sheloch and warned him that if Sheloch constinued his provocations , he would kill him.

The headman , told him that he would hold a meeting for the eldery men of the hamlet and ask Sheloch to cease his provactive actions.

When the meeting was convened. Abu Maqt addressed Dhughayyem saying: "O, Dhughayyem!you should know that we are not living in a forest. Dhughayyem said angerily : "hold you horses " But Abu maqt said loudly and harshly:" I shall divorce you from your mother! " Dhughayem said : Shut up or I'll blow off your head at once ! " then he called his brother Salbud to go to Bu Serhan and ask him to bring his camels to transport their effects to leave the hamlet for good."

Then Bu Saleh , a respectable old man : rebuked Abu Maqt and asked him to aopoloiize for the bad phrase he uttered: Abu Maqt , stepped forward to Dhughayyem and said:" accursed is the Satan, It is a tongue slip my Cousin.' And he was about to cry tears flowing down his cheeks; he uttered a crying sound like;" Bua'a Bua' a. Seeing BuMaqt crying, Dhughayyem calmed down . The headman said: " Execuse me gentlemen , no body should talk withhout my permission. Let me remind you of the Prophet's saying:, (PBH), ' He who believes in Allah and The Last Day should say ' goodwords or remain silent!'"

The headman called on Dhughayyem to present his pretex for taking the sesam from Sheloch by force:

Dhughayyem said:"Gentlemen , you already know that Shelock had tried to provoke me several times. The last time was when he incited he artisain not to bleach my pots, . yesterday: he accused my nephews, Zeid and Muhajer, of stealing his sesame when he gave it to them as a present. They are here now and you can ask them to tell you the story. The head man aksed the boys to tell what happened.

Muhajer stood up and said:" yesterday afternoon, I was playing with my cousin Ziad; Shelock called us and asked us our names . then he told us that he had two small bags full of sesame and he wanted to send them as presents for our families. We took the two bags and left him. Suddenly he came on his horse and he was shouting that we hd stolen some sesame from his stack yard. Some people gathred around us , among them was my uncle Dhughayyem who noticed that the bags were firmly closed with thread and needle. We cannot do that. He accused us of something we did not do. Zeid also stood and he told the same story Then Dhughayyem said : "how do you explain Shelock's action?'" The men were surprised and most of them blamed Sheloch for accusing the childen of stealing the sasame when he give it to them.

Sheloch stood up and siad:" I do admit it that I tricked the two boys to take the sesame. In fact , it was the Satan that tempted me to behave so. I had not forgotten the four sheep that I gave to Dhughayyem and he did not take them ; he gave them to the old woman . he humilated me. I know it's been bad to behave like hat.Therefore ,I do grant Dhughayyem   all the seasme he took from me last night . I freely do this. I am the one who had committed that mistakey , therefore , I genuely ask him to forgive me. I do here promise I shall never ever commit any provacative actions aginst him or any member of his family.

Dhughayyem siad :" God will for give you , but I warn you never try to provoke me."The headman intervened and said :" please Dhughayyem ! Accept his apology and we all witness that he promised that he shall never commit any provocative actions aginst you or any member of your family." Dhughayyem accepted his apology .and the problem was over.

Hadjis was pleased with Muhajer who was   more eloquent than Zeid when he delivered his witness against Sheloch. Two days lator, Dhughayyem and Salbud took the sesame to Nabuls and sold it there for eighty dinars. When they came back . They went the head man and told him that they sold the sesme for eighty Dinars. They gave him forty dinars to give them to Sheloch. The headman said that he would give ten dinars of them to Umm Ahmad, the old woman. And he added that he would distrube the rest to needy people after informing Shelock.

CHAPTER-SIX

The year 1960 was the time for Muhajer to go to school as he was   almost nine years old though he had a stature   that made him look older . He was tall and strong. He looked as if he were twelve years old. Hadjis and Rifqa had decided not to send him to school. They wanted him to be a sheep shepherd when he would reach the age of twelve years. But when Muhajer terrified the thieves, they decided to send him to school, hoping him bright future. So they had to move from Wazeer hamlet to Munqatta'a where the school was. When Jababr's family moved to Munqatta'a , they did not have a house there. Therefore, they had to live in a tent pitched near a spring of water adjoining a hill surrounded by a grove of huge fig trees. The place was about two miles from the Munqatta'a preparatory school established by the UNRWA. Faruq, the eldest son had join his family after he left his grandmother.

On the first day of school, the boy was accompanied by his father and his elder brother who was in grade- three that year. It was a new wondrous world to Muhajer. There were many boys at the school. They were dressed in an attire different from the little cloak or dishdasha. Every boy wore a shirt and trousers; the shirts were white and the trousers were khaki   and the shoes were black. One huge boy dressed in an olive colored second-hand military uniform and he had old black military boots and he covered his head with a yellow head cover taken from the national guard! That boy was called "the beetle." This boy was over seventeen years of age. The principal of the school assigned him to help the class teacher .The class room was overcrowded with boys , all of them had their heads shaved with razor blades and because of the heat in the room that had little ventilation , drops of sweat were trickling down the boys' faces and necks. The pupils endured the heat but they were trembling of fear stemming from two sources; the prefect of the class, the beetle ' and the class teacher whose name was Antar. He was named after the famous pre – Islamic knight in pre-Islamic Arabia. The prefect was given authorities to discipline pupils. He would carry a stick and wave it in the air to frighten the children and with his harsh voice, he would shout to them asking them to keep silent! The ones who were troublemakers had their names Written on the chalkboard with multiplication signs against their names. Each multiplication sign meant that the trouble -maker deserved five slaps or lashes with teacher's rod. In fact,   the teachers would use corporal punishment. Trouble makers were punished with a bamboo cane: the teacher would occasionally beat the pupil's buttocks ruthlessly. with a number of whips according the multiplication sings; the number of the whips was never less than fifteen! At the beginning of the school, the pupils used to have new shoes, but when two moths would have passed, nearly all the pupils would go with bare feet. The bare- feet would dangle from the high seats. It was rare to see a pupil wearing shoes. Most of the pupils especially those whose families took care of sheep would come to school either on foot or raining donkeys. Those who go the school on foot would step on sharp thorns that would pierce the soles of their feet and remain there forming a hard skin layer densely paved with thorns. Most pupils would have upper skin of their fee chapped during winter. Though it was an indication of miserable life, the children liked to have that shield that protected them from the painful bamboo lashes when some teachers would hit their feet in the falaka.

One day. Muhajer's name was written on the chalkboard. so he had to be flogged in the fourth period when the class teacher would come to punish the trouble-makers. There was a recess for thirty minutes before the fourth period. The schoolchildren would be free to leave the school and buy their breakfast from the nearby shops. Fearing the punishment by the class teacher, Muhajer left the school at once and hid in a wide cornfield behind the school. He did not go to school for five consecutive days. He would hide in that field in the morning and stay until the school day was over, then he would go home with his brother saying to him that he was in the cornfield checking a skylark nest there! His parents did not notice that he was absent for a whole week! The principal of the school summoned his elder brother, Faruq, and asked him to tell his father to report to the school for an urgent matter!

The next day, Hadjis went to Principal's office and was surprised when the principal told him that his son, Muhajer, had been absent from school for more than a week! Hadjis assured the Principal that his son went to school every day: he told the principal that he left home in the morning with his brother for the school. The principal sent for Faruq , who told them that Muhajer came with him in the morning , but before

reaching the school, he told him that he wanted to go into the corn field behind the school to check the nest of a skylark there! The principal sent for the prefect of the class and one of the janitors of the school and asked them to go and check the cornfield. They went at once. When they were about to enter the corn field, the Beetle told the janitor to wait and called out:

"Muhajer ! We know that you are there, come out at once, or you will be lashed with the whip you know!"

The little boy came out shivering of fear and walked with the two men to school! When they got to the office of the principal, the boy started crying loudly and saying: " for God's sake don't beat me! Don't beat me!" Antar, the teacher of the class, was boiling with anger. So without thinking, he stopped the boy and slapped his face. The child fell down rolling on the floor!

Seeing his son rolling with pain on the floor of the room, Hadjis swiftly hit Antar with his cane on his tall neck. The teacher jumped out of a window. Hadjis said: "Now you fly through the widow as you forced Fayyadh's son to jump out of the window of the class room two days ago." Some uproar and clamor coincided with that event. The principal hurried to the main gate of the school where he met with a crowd of people shouting: "where is Antar? Let him come out! Let him come out!" A few moments later, three young men came to the crowd dragging someone on the dusty ground of the yard beyond the wall of the school and one of them said: "Here you are! This is Antar , the criminal." The crowd stampeded him and spitted on him and cursed him !There was no body to help him , the teaching staff stood aloof! In fact, some of them   said: "It serves him right. He is a trouble-maker." The crowd did not disperse until some of the knights of the police force arrived at the scene. The crowd were from the Fayyadh's son tribe. Antar had broken his arm and forced him to jump through the window earlier in the week.

Antar had his left arm broken as he was beaten heavily by the crowd and he felt pain in his chest. Some of his ribs were aching too. His scalp of his skull was full of swelling bruises, too. It was difficult to pinpoint the culprits. The crowd was of a great number. When the crowd dispersed, he principal of the school asked the refugee pupils to leave school and never come back again! Some of the students who were teen agers dared to ask the principal the reason. The principal said that the crowd that attacked the teacher were from the refugees especiallythe desert men (Bedouins) of the southern desert of Palestine !As of that day the refugee children should not be allowed to school ! The principal asked the refugees' children not to come to school until further notice. Most of the boys rejoiced as they were released at that early time of the day! Two hours of peace elapsed - it was calm before storm!

Then, the tracks and roads leading to the school were busy with moving people on horses, donkeys and mules. Some people were riding camels; they all poured into the main dusty road leading to the school. Clouds of dust were rising from the dusty tracks. The parents rushed to school together at a time. When they reached there, they began shouting: " You idiot! You idiot! Come out, come out!" The principal rushed to the main gate of the school and asked them what they wanted ; the answer was :"You and Antar, leave this place immediately ! You are no longer wanted here! This is not the school of your parents. If you refuse, we shall uproot you as we uproot trees out of the soil! Open the gate!" The principal said that Antar had left the village and gone home for treatment of his broken ribs and he had filed an official complaint at the police station against the mobs who attacked him. The crowd shouted that the school should be closed for all. The claimed that the teachers lived among the villagers who became friends of them. The teachers were biased towards the children of the village. They would sympathize with them! The school should be closed for all villagers and refugees! The crowd demanded. The boys inside the classrooms crowded at the windows of the classrooms looking at the main gate; they saw and heard what was going on! Some of them rushed to the doors of the school. The situation was out of control! The principal was not able to appease the anger of the crowd. Some young men of the crowd jumped over the gate, ran towards the office of the principal, and set fire to the office! Seeing that his office was in flames, the principal fled from the window of the back room behind his office and he ran away towards the police station. Some villagers ran their horses and told the police what was going on!

The force of the police station with their commander arrived at the scene after some villagers told them that the school was under attack. They started dispersing the crowd and they were able to detain a few of them. The police did not release the detainees until peace and order were observed.

The principal of the school and the teachers complained to the police requesting that this case should be settled at court. The commander of the police saw that taking the matter to court was not wise. His superiors might blame him for the insecurity and disorder in the village. Therefore, he acted swiftly. He summoned the notable men of the tribe (refugees of a tribe of Bedouins of the Southern part of Palestine) and told them that the teachers of the school wanted to sue them and if they won the case, the tribe would pay a heavy price! He advised them to settle the case amicably and reach an agreement! If they agreed to compromise, he would release the detainees from the tribe. Meanwhile his assistant convinced the teachers of the school to compromise. The principal of the school believed that the teacher who had beaten the boys could lose his job if the parents of the students reported his unacceptable practices to the headquarters of UNRWA.

Thus, the commander of the police station was able reach a settlement between the two parties-the attackers and the schoolteachers. He had the principal as well as the chieftain of the tribe sign written undertakings that they would never resort to violence to solve problems arising at the school.In addition, they would not break the rules and regulations of education at   the UNRWA schools! The teachers insisted that the villagers sign the same undertakings.

Muhajer psychological problems remained unsolved: He would wake up at night crying and shouting: "Don't beat me! Don't beat me for God's sake!." Sometimes, he would cry all the night; I don't want school. At last his parents decided that he should not go to school that year! Therefore, Hadjis went to the school and talked to the principal about his son's case. The principal suggested that Muhajer could join school the coming year! The child should be given a chance to forget his misery that year, because he thought the child might forget what

Happened and he would recommend the transfer of the teacher from that school.

Thinking of what had happened at the school, the commander of the police station realized that event not only endangered the teaching staff but it would have risked his position and all the police force, had the case aggravated. Had it been reported to higher authorities, in that case, he would have been charged of negligence of his duty to observe that the village was under control? He thought if   the school had been nearer to the police station, the riot would not have aggravated because the rioters would not dare to attack the school under the nose of the police. To avoid similar incidents in the future, the school should be nearer to the police station. Therefore, he surprised the head man of the village   with a visit; he went to the headman's home .with two horsemen of the force. The headman welcomed them with apprehension fearing that there was something urgent. After dinner, the commander talked to the headman and he suggested that the school be transferred to a site nearer to the police station. He said he was afraid that the case would take place again as the refugees   threatened that one day, they would take revenge on the teachers of the school for maltreatment of their children. He believed they were serious, because it is well known that the Bedouins never forget their revenge; they would revenge and retaliate even if a long time had elapsed. There is an adage: "A Bedouin took his revenge upon his foe after forty years had elapsed and he said I antedated the revenge. ". Therefore, he would be grateful to the headman and the inhabitants if they allocate a piece of land for building a new school. He suggested that the land should be nearer to the police station. He advised them to allocate the piece of land between the Ottoman Detention Station, the police station, and the village.The headman went with police commander and saw the piece of land which turned out that it belonged to the headman himself. Therefore, a committee of the villagers was formed and a group of them went to higher authorities and asked them to move the school there. A year later, a new school building was established. It consisted of 15 large classrooms and a wing of three large halls for the administration.   The school consisted of two parallel rows of rooms with a distance of about thirty meters wide separating the two rows.

A year passed during which Muhajer's little mind could not absorb how his father could protect him, his mother , the shepherd and his sheep from the wild ferocious beasts of the wilderness when he was not able to protect him from that demon of the school!. The new building of the school was built by the help of the UNRWA. The school was more spacious than old one.

When Muhajer would burst into crying at night, his father would remember a line of verse he learned from the commander of his company of the National Guard. Hadjis would be heard rehearsing the line as if he were singing it:

"A wolf howled while I was alone

I felt safe , but when a man shouted was horrified

So one day, Hadjis went to school and met the principal who advised him to stop sending the boy to school that year and he should give him enough time to forget the bad accident he had undergone at school!

The boy spent that year at home. One day Hadjis saddled his mule , took some water and had Muhajer mount the mule. Hadjis held the rope of mule and. said that he was going to spend the day at his grove; he wanted to check if the seedlings he planted last year had grown or not. The boy was anxious to go there. He had not seen the grove for more than a year. It was a clear morning. When they reached the grove, they entered from the opening at the southern eastern angle of the wall border of the grove. Muhajer rejoiced when he saw the boughs of the trees moving gently in the breezes , they looked like if they became happy with presence of Muhjaer and Hadjis .

Hadjis asked Muhajer to fetch the tea kettle from the cavern. He unloaded the mule and kindled fire to prepare tea for breakfast. The smoke of the fire soared high in the sky.

While Muhajer was coming back to Hadjis , he noticed a man entering the grove from the opening. To his surprise, it was Halabi, Abu Sha-ma. So   Muhajer shouted to Hadjis ;" Look! Look! Who is there ! It's Halabi Abu fuss!(Literally father of the fart!) . Hearing the boy, Halabi turned back and walked towards the opening. Hadjis was embarrassed! He shouted to the man:" Come back! Bu Sha_ma !Come back! Don't take him seriously! . He is only a child without discretion! Come back! I want to have a deal with you." Bu Sha-ma came back, and said: "You are to blame! You haven't brought him to be polite" Hadjis smiled and said: "Don't blame him. He was an eye witness to what had happened and he has never forgotten it." He added

"Come on have a cup of tea with us and we are going to have breakfast. Come on! Help yourself! Eat with usTake it easy, man! It happens even in the most regulated families. Come on! Help yourself!"

After breakfast. Bu Shama asked Hadjis what he wanted.

Hadjis said:" I want to have a deal with you. You know I am living now at Munqatta'a and it is difficult for me to come here daily to take care of the grove. So I would like you to take care of my olive grove and you take its product of oil or your work on it. . Take its product I do not need it all. I need only eighty liters of oil. You know that I have over 600 trees and all of them are fruitful. Take care of the grove. Don't allow goats to graze on it. Dig the land under the trees and carry out all the necessary tasks to preserve and sustain the growth of the trees. You can live in the cavern. I'll give you the hunting rifle! Keep the grove clean of weeds."Halabi agreed and was pleased. He promised to give Hadjis his share of oil by the end of November after three months of that time !

The man left happily. Muhajer went to the shade of the old Carob tree he used to play under. He began collecting small stones to construct his miniature house! He was surprised by Hadjis who started beating his back with a knob stick. The child began yelling. His yelling reverberated the whole area with its dales and hills. Bu Shama heard the yelling of the boy and came back panting. He was very tired from ascending the steep slope. He begged Hadjis not to beat the boy!

The dry crusts of the scars on the back of the boy were bleeding. Blood pervaded the garment of the boy. It was statured with blood. He began weeping; he was helpless with no body to protect him after Halabi went away. Hadjis resumed beating the boy. While the boy was crying loudly, there were loud explosions in the clear sky as two aircraft were flying high in the sky with two jets of white smoke after them. They broke the sound barrier one after another. Hadjis was terrified by the roar and the explosions. He stopped beating the boy and they both hurried going back home.

When they came back home in the evening, Rifqa was pleased to see the boy's garment tarnished with blood. She asked "How was it boy! You enjoyed it! It serves you right." Muhajer said:' Mother! My father hit with a stick!" Rifqa interrupted him saying: "Don't call me mother, I am not your mother shut up!" Hadjis addressed her;' you shut up! We are his parents and you are his mother in spite of you, understand?"

When the first of September came again. Mahjer had to go back to school. This year his sister who was 18 months younger than him, went with him in the same class. He was annoyed when she asked permission loudly that she wanted to go the bath room to pass water! She said literally: (I want to pass water!) The kids burst into laughing, this matter embarrassed Muhajer very much and at the long recess between the third and fourth period, he left school and ran home; he arrived homepanting and sweating! Then he started crying and shouting; "I'll never go to School!"

When asked why, he said:" your daughter brought shame on me! All the boys were laughing at me! She openly asked the teacher's permission to the bath room to pass water! Now Hadjis was anxious to see the girl who arrived two hours later. He asked her what she said to the teacher and how she said it : she told that truth she said :" I asked him to allow me to go to the bathroom because I wanted to pass water !" "Did the boys laugh, then?" Hadjis asked. She answered that they did! So, Hadjis used his cane and wiped her three times, and firmly said :"no school for you! Girls should not be taught with boys. If there were a school for girls, you would go then don't go to school." Muhajer was pleased to hear this!

In the morning of the next day, Hadjis went to the school with his son, to ask the teacher to forgive Muhajer for the

classes he missed yesterday! The teacher was kind enough; was a man who treated children with kindness and compassion! He smiled to the boy and went into the teacher's room and brought a box of candies, opened it and offered the boy some candies. The boy was pleased and went happily to his class! Hadjis told the teacher about Antra's harsh treatment of children last year. The teacher promised Hadjis that he would treat the boy kindly and he would exert his best efforts to teach him well.

Four months later, in a warm morning, Hadjis was passing by the school.In front the school, there were about thirty pupils sitting on the thick mallow grass, with their teacher having a portable chalkboard leaned at the wall of the school fence. He had already written the reading text on the board. He called on Hadjis to see how good at reading Muhajer was . He asked Muhajer to stand up and read the lesson back ward beginning from the last word of the line at the bottom. Muhajer read the text without any errors. The pupils applauded him. Hadjis thanked the teacher and left happily!

Hadjis realized how the kind treatment was fruitful. Education cannot be achieved well with harsh treatment, so he

said to himself that he would amend his treatment of his family, his wife, and the children.

The school new site was safer. It adjoined the police station with a barbed fence between them. No intruder would venture to carry any action of sabotage to the school.

The principal thought of making the school an officially mixed school for boys and girls. The highest-class level was the third preparatory class at the school. That meant that the students in the school were children whose ages were less than sixteen. The number of girls in the school was meager and there was no school for girls at the village. He went to the headman's guesthouse and met with a few of the villagers. He was specialized in Islamic law, he had studied it at the teachers' institute for two years. He said that girls had the right to go to school; Islam encouraged education of women and Muslims should act according to the teachings of their religion . The villagers were not satisfied with his suggestion at first. However, he was clever. He said in another meeting:

"If sending girls to the centers of districts away from the village where there were special schools for girls to study there, it was more comfortable for their daughters to study with boys of their village who know them and know their families.To convince the villagers of what he was saying, he told them horrible stories about secrete gangs who would kidnap girls who were away from their homes! They killed them and drained their blood and sold it. That happened   to a girl in the city where his family lived. He knew the news last week when he visited his family on the weekend. The parents whose daughters were studying away from them were terrified and asked him how they could solve the problem of their daughters.

He promised them to help them by absorbing their daughters at the school of the village! He convinced some of the villagers whose daughters were studying at the centers of the districts away from the village.

A week later a few of the girls were transferred to the school, the boys were astonished to see girls studying with them. The oldest girl of them was called Nad-dah who was in the third preparatory class. The boys of the village felt embarrassed to see a girl of their village among strange boys, not from the village. So they began teasing her. One of them was nicknamed The Joker but the popular nickname for him was the He- goat. . He was dubbed as the He- goat, for repeating several times the grade

levels at school. , he had already repeated the sixth grade for three times, when he failed the grade for the third time .the certificate carried the comment: " His result is "a failure but as he overused his right of failing the grade , he has been promoted to the higher level- grade ." This He-goat began a resistance movement against absorbing girls at the school. He initiated his resistance movement by inserting into the drawer of Nad-dah's seat an empty chalk box but filled with stool! When sitting at her seat, the girl could not tolerate the bad smell permeating the room; she looked for the source of the smell. She located the box and told the principal of the school who sent a janitor to take it out. In fact, the principal went to the class and noticed a few Arabic words written in pencil on the lid of the box the spelling was wrong: "Welcome! Greeting to you in our school,

your love !" on the other side of the box inscribed was the real name of He-goat."

The He-goat was summoned to the office of the principal who sent him to call his father and he also sent the girl home to call her father. Both parents came at the same time. The principal told them the story; the girl's father insisted that the He-goat be punished. The He - goat was standing near the door , when he realized that the case was serious , he   ran out of the door like a md march hare and ran home ; he tricked his mother into giving him some money, claiming that his father needed it. He ran away from home and went to hide among thick trees east of the village. He waited for the bus that took him to the nearest city. (At that time he was more than seventeen years old!) The resistance movement against girls studying with boys had disappeared with the He-goat absence from the scene!

The following year about thirty girls who were studying outside the village joined the school officially and the school became a mixed school for girls and boys! There was no water system in the village. Women, especially the young ones, would go to the spring to fill buckets of water and take them home. They would usually go to the spring in groups.

They had to carry the buckets of water on their heads this entailed that they had to walk slowly lest they spill the water on themselves. To protect their heads they used thick cloth round rings on their heads under the buckets of water.

They were beautiful girls and the young men were tempted to take strolls at the tracks of the girls going to the spring. Two bothersome thick-skinned young men caused a lot of embarrassment to the girls on the way to the spring. One day, they both went to the city and came back wearing new Arabian cloaks of the same cloth and the same color. They seemed to show off their new garments and they wanted to impress the girls with them.

They would not talk to the girls, but they would obstruct the narrow track by not giving room for the girls to walk freely. Therefore, an old man thought of a solution for the problem: He went to the city in the morning and came back in the afternoon. The sun was about to set. Therefore, he put a cushion on his donkey. Riding the donkey, the old man went to the spring taking the main track leading to the spring. Scores of girls were walking slowly towards the spring; the two annoying young men wearing their new cloaks were going there, too. The old man let his donkey walk slowly after the two young men, suddenly, the girls burst into hysterical fits of laughing! They startled the two young men who looked back; they saw the old man on his donkey. The girls continued laughing, but the two young men did not know the reason for their laughing! When they looked at the girls as if they were asking why the girls were laughing, one of the girls pointed with here forefinger to the cloth of the donkey's cushion. The two young men were shocked to see that the cloth of the donkey's cushion was the same cloth of their cloaks. They felt shameful and they left the place at once. They would never take a stroll in that track again!

The school day would finish by one o'clock every week day. The teachers of the school were living in hired houses in the village. They had no cars they used to walk to school. They would take a dusty track that led to the school, but at the same time, this track led to the water spring. The girls of the village liked to go to bring water at the time the school day ended. Muhajer took to a teacher who walked with him when they left school. The teacher was a handsome man. He was about twenty-five years old. One of the girls,(Wardeh) who used to go the spring would come across the teacher on her way to the spring. As he was a stranger to her, she could not talk to him. The women of the village were not allowed to talk with men in the streets. The young woman at that time could not stand with her brother in the street. This was to prevent rumors about her honor!

The girl was attached to the teacher. They would exchange smiles when they met in the middle of the road. She was blond with beautiful and wide that looked like

two almond shape jewels glittering with hope beneath her crescent black eye brows that seemed to be drawn with pencil.

One day, she called Muhajer asked him what the name of the teacher was. He said his name was Sami. She asked Muhajer inscribe the teacher' name in the shape of flower the teacher's name on the white handkerchief she was carrying with her. Two weeks later; while she was going to the spring, she saw the teacher approaching her from the opposite side; she drew his attention with the white handkerchief, then dropped it to the ground. The teacher picked it up and continued walking home. The next day, he asked Muhajer to take a letter from him and he asked him to read it for her. Muhajer, was a clever boy; he asked the teacher to read it for him so that he would read it correctly for her. The teacher read the letter and let Muhajer read it. Then, the teacher warned Muhajer that if he told anyone about the letter, he would fail the subjects he was teaching him that year! Muahjer promised not to tell anybody. While Muhajer was standing with the teacher, a woman who was dubbed The Owl saw them.It was a curious woman who liked to know everything. She called Muhajer when he left the teacher and asked him what the teacher gave him . At first Muhajer hesitated to tell her, but when the woman told him that she would tell his father about what happened. He trembled with fear. Then, he told her the truth! The Owl smiled to the child, tapped gently on his shoulder, and asked him to cool down. She went to the kitchen, brought a box of Turkish delight, and gave him some to eat. Then he read the letter for her. It read:

My dear love Warden;

Thank you for the nice handkerchief that you embroidered my name with small beads on it . I love you very much; you live in the deepest core of my heart. I will soon bring my mother to the village and ask her to go your father's house and ask your hand for me.

So long my love! Your love forever
Sami

The owl was boiling   at heart but outwardly, she showed off happiness. She told Muhajer to keep it secret and not tell anybody about it. She promised him that she would come at night and go with him to give the letter to Wradeh.

When Muhajer arrived home, his father asked him why he was late. He said that The Owl called him to her house and offered him some Turkish delight. To this , Hadjis got very angry . He started kicking the boy with his heavy boot. Muhajer began yelling. Then Hadjis hit the boy with a knob stick on his head . the blood gushed at once. While that trouble was taking place, The owl was knocking on the door. Rifqa welcomed her but, telling her that Hadjis was angry with the boy because he came home late.

Then the owl leered her eyes towards Hadjis saying to him:" Shame on you! You show off your virility by beating this child. Go to Safi and show off your virility there. His daughter, wardeh, is making your son , Muhajer, a love courier for her and Sami, the teacher.

Jabbaer asked: "what did you say? Repeat, I couldn't catch up with you. Would you please repeat that?" She said:" When I have a cup of tea I will tell you the truth." Drinking the cup of tea, the Owl said to Hadjis :"Check your son's book bag. There is a letter inside it." Hadjis checked the bag and brought out the letter. He asked Muhajer to read it . Muhajer read the letter. The owl laughed and commented:" shame on you ,Muhajer, son of the big wig! You don't feel ashamed of yourself to be a procurer for whores and rogues!" Rifqa commented angrily; " look! you , owl! You know who the procurers are. They are you and the likes! Why don't you ask yourself why people call you The Owl?"

To this the owl started weeping And asked Hadjis :" "Do you like what your wife says. She istarnishing my reputation. Shame on you I thought you were a real man!' Infuriated, Hadjis shouted to her:" get up and go to hell, you are accursed! Never enter this house again! Rise up, go to hell, you owl of bad omen! Get the hell out of here! "The Owl rushed out. Then Hadjis followed her, throwing some old shoes on her!

A few minute later Hadjis took Muhajer by the hand telling him not to be afraid. He took the boy with him carrying the the school bag. And they went to Wardeh's house. He called out "Safi, Safi" Safi was an old man in his sixties, came out limping, but his three young sons came out at once. They welcomed Hadjis and asked him to go in. But he angrily and haughtily said:" I will not step on your rug unless you prove to me that you are real men who wear their head rings slanted on their heads." The three young men jumped at his throat and started beating him. Their father loudly rebuked them. He firmly asked them to refrain from beating the man saying: "Stop it, the man is at our home." The young men stopped beating Hadjis . Muhajer had a role in the clash: He started threw some stones at the three men grazing the skin above the eyebrows of one of the young men. The old man held Hadjis by the arm and begged him to go inside. When they went inside the guest room,   Safi offered Hadjis some coffee. . Then Hadjis told them the story and showed them the letter. The three young men remained calm, but they sneaked out of the room one after another. A few minutes later, noises and clamor came out of the adjacent room. The three young men began beating Wardeh. Leaving her helpless; they hurried out of the main gate of the house. An hour later, loud shouts were heard at the haystack yard. Of the village. The three young men went to Sami's house and called him out. He went out to them. They lured him to the haystack yard where they started beating him with their heavy knob sticks. They rained him with hard beatings and strikes. A crowd of people hurried to the place and watched the three young men beating the teacher at the haystack yard. One of them was repeating averse   of   poetry:
" The Nobel honor cannot be saved from hurt unless blood is shed at its fringes!" he added:" Write love letters , you bustard! You do not know that there are men here! We are not communists. We are conservatives not bolshevists! Know this well. We are villagers who keep their honor clean. We will erase your memory if you stay here! You will not live long at this village. Tomorrow before the sun rises you should leave this village!"

The next day the whole village knew the story as The Owl who was a bad news-bearer transmitted the news to all people there. The owl was disposed to inciting social disorder among the inhabitants.

The next morning the teacher left the village with the first bus going to the nearest city. The principal of the school called Muhajer to his office and knew the story from him. The Principal modified the timetable of the classes and the school leaving time to prevent any contact with girls going the spring water.

A few weeks later a group of men and women of Sami's folk, among them was his mother, came to Safi's home to ask for Wardeh's hand in marriage to Sami.Safi turned them down. The pretext was that Wardeh had recently been engaged to her cousin, (the He-goat.) And they were going to get married soon.

Two days later, Safi left the village heading for Jerusalem. He went to bring back the He-goat, his nephew, to the village. He had his address from a soldier from the village who had already met the He- goat and took his address from him. When the He-goat left the village, he worked as a construction worker. The work was very difficult for him, so he looked for a suitable job for him and finally he was employed by a private school as a janitor. His work usually started at seven and ended at tree in the afternoon. He was surprised to see his uncle coming to visit him. As the He –goat was living in misery with other workers like him in an overcrowded domicile; he went with his uncle to a cheap hotel for the night. There they had dinner, and after dinner, Safi, told his nephew, the He-goat, the story of Wardeh and Sami, the stranger. The He-goat got very nervous upon hearing the story. His uncle said he came to the He –goat to rescue the family's reputation which had become mud at the hands of Muhajer and the owl who spread the story throughout the village. Safi elated the He –goat by playing on his pride. He said that when the He- goat left the village, there were not enough men to guard the dignity of the village.The He- goat affected tension and insisted to go to the village at once. They news brought by his uncle filled his heart with grudge against Muhajer` and the Owl. Swelled- headed, the He-goat convinced his uncle that they should go to their village once. They took a taxi and arrived the village at dawn.

Before taking the taxi, they both went to a confectioner's store where they bought abundant quantity of Turkish delight and other sweets for the He- goat and Wardeh's wedding party. The He-goat's mother was pleased to see him coming home back.

In the evening the coffee pounder sounded at Safi's house,. Men gathered at Safi's hosting room. And one of his sons went to the marriage officer inviting him to solemnize the marriage of Wardeh and the He- got. The most surprised person was Wardeh , who started weeping. The marriage officer should make sure that Wardeh had not been forced to   marry the He – goat.   Before he filled the marriage-contract form, he asked her father's permission to ask her some questions pertaining to marriage. The marriage officer went with her father to the adjacent room where Wardeh was sitting on a sofa. One of her brothers was outside the room standing in place where she could see him through the door. The Imam asked her if she agreed to marry the He- goat. The girl was about to say" no!" when she noticed her brother waving his revolver in his right hand as a threatening sign. She said that she agreed to get married to the He- goat and said that nobody intimidated or coerced her to accept marrying him. . It was Sunday night when Safai announced that he would hold the marriage party on the coming Friday.

On Monday, the He-goat left home early in the morning and he waited for Muhajer on the track to the north of the village. Muhajer was going to school . It was around seven o'clock when the He goat appeared from behind a tree .he shouted to Muhajer to stop . As he was shouting, a policeman heard the shouting and saw the He -goat intercept the boy's road. The police officer was taking care of his horse near the barbed fence separating the school from the police station. He was about forty meters away from both of them.   Realizing that the He-got was going to attack him, Muhajer swiftly picked up a stone, waited for the He-goat to approach him, and at a proper distance he hurled the stone towards the He-goat. The stone struck him directly between his eyebrows. Blood gushed at once flowing down into his eyes; he was not able to see. Outraged, the He-goat began running towards Muhajer though he was not able to see clearly.

He tumbled over with a huge stone protruding out in the middle of the track. So, Muhajer was terrified and hurried back to his home. He ran fast and reached home panting. When his parents saw him panting, they asked him what it was. He told them that the He- goat   prevented him from going to school; he was about to beat him with a huge stick he was carrying. He added that he struck The He- goat with a stone between his two eyebrows.

A few minutes later, Hadjis went to the police station and filed an official complaint against the He- goat.

Two police officers brought the He- goat to the police station and detained him there. Two hours later,Hadjis, Muhajer, Safi and the headman of the village arrived at the police station. The headman went into the office of the commander of the station and begged him to solve the problem amicably. He said that he convinced Hadjis to forgive the He-goat and Safi, his uncle, agreed to reconcile with Muhajer and his father. He added that the He-goat was not serious in intimidating the boy and he was going to be married on the coming Friday. The commander said that there was a common law to be observed and adhered to. The commander insisted that he should cross-examine the He –goat and teach him that the common -law must be observed. The commander came out and began asking Muhajer first.

He asked the boy; "Why did you not go to school?" The boy answered; "The He- goat intimated me and I was afraid of him. He was about to attack me with a knob stick, but I defended myself by throwing a stone at him." The He-goat said loudly "This boy is a liar! Do not believe him. I will not let a small boy like this hit me. He is a liar I did not intimidate him nor did I shout to him." A policeman was standing there said firmly:" You are the liar, I heard you shouting to the boy and I saw you hurrying towards him. He struck you with a stone defending himself." To this the He -goat said abruptly:" Shut up your mouth and bite a shoe!"

The commander at once cuffed the He –goat's face twice and angrily ordered three of his men to take him to the hay- stack area to the east of village and flog him with a hundred stripes there in public!

Safi, was dismayed and embarrassed by the conduct of his nephew so he said: "The one who dubbed you a He-goat was utterly right. You have brought shame on me and you are spoiling everything! Your wedding will be on Friday. Won't it be?" The headman begged the commander to release the He-goat. The commander agreed to do so, but insisted that he should teach him a lesson before he released him.

Before taking the He- goat to the hay stack yard, the commander had the He -goat and his uncle, Safi sign a warranty, that the He-goat shall not hurt Muhajer or any member of his family and he should not resort to settling problems by intimidation or coercion.

When they reached the hay-stack area to the east of the village , two horse men laid the He- goat at his back on the ground and raised his feet by a long thick stick that held the ropes that were used to hold his feet tightly together during the Falaka .

Two police officers started flogging the He-goat feet ruthlessly. There were many people witnessing the event,. All of them felt pity on the He-goat except one person: it was the owl who was pleased to see him being punished. She shouted happily: "It serves you right. It serves you right. She began ululating The He-goat painfully said;" shut up bitch.! , you will feel sorry one day!" The commander, asked the two men to stop after the men had beaten his feet eighty times. They released the He–goat. However, he fell to the ground. As he got up! He was not able to walk. Two of his cousins brought a donkey and had him ride the donkey. The owl said: "This is a wonderful sight! A he-goat riding a donkey. "

Safi and the headman went to Hadjis's house and begged him to forgive the He- goat. They brought a present to Muhajer and gave him some money . They assured Hadjis that the He- goat should never try to hurt the boy.

Therefore, there would be several consecutive nights of rejoice and happiness. People of the village, the elderly, young men and young women, would gather in an open area in a spacious open yard in front of Safi's house to celebrate the marriage of the He–goat. The celebration nights were held there,

Because the He-goat's father had passed away two years ago. So it was his uncle's duty to patronize the marriage. So he had the celebration nights and the wedding day be at his house. As there was no electricity in the village during those days, Safi used twelve kerosene lanterns to light the area every night. .The young men of the Bedouins encampments near the village would come in groups to take part in the celebrations. While they were marching towards the celebration place, they would chant:

O! girl standing on the roofs.

Come and see our actions

You pride on your hair

But we pride on our actions

The young men would form large semi- circle, connecting together but horizontally extending both arms and dance the dabkah. The dabkah had a leader who would organize the movement of the dancers' feet. They were very organized and agile. The dabkah was accompanied by flute tunes, and sometimes double piped flute, besides the singing of one of the people dancing.

One night, Yasen, the He-goat proved that he was a really idiot he-goat. The dabkah was going smoothly and it was very organized; no body of the dancers was inconsistent .The He-goat squeezed himself between two of the dancers in the semi-circle and without following the instructions of the leader and the tunes of the flute, he haphazardly began beating the ground with his heavy old military boots rapidly and consecutively. He caused a cloud of dust to rise to the eyes of the dancers. Under the faint light and with cloud of dust over enveloping the place ,the dancers , the dancers looked like tomb stones popping up and down through the dust They at once stopped dancing, but the He-goat remained dancing   unaware that he was left dancing alone. The Owl who was watching was vexed and shouted to him to stop ,but he continued. A young man said to the owl: "Leave him alone, he is automated,; he will be put off by himself!"

Friday came and the ceremonial dinner was scheduled at two o'clock in the afternoon. The invitees arrived in groups after ten o'clock. There were three huge big tents joined together to form a large saloon. The floor of the tent was furnished with wool mattresses laid over Arabian rugs. They were hand – woven by the women of the village.

The majority of the invitees came on horses- pure Arabian horses. The ceremony tent for receiving the invitees was pitched at an open area to the east of the village. To express their joy, the invitees had horse races. The sight was spectacular: equestrians would compete in groups of two , three, or seven. The horses competing would be of various colors. Meanwhile circles of dabkah continued till the banquet was ready. While the invitees were having the ceremony dinner, the young men took the He–goat to bathe him!. The He- goat said that he had already had the bath, and came out wearing the wedding suit- a black suit made from Held wool and he was wearing white shirt but he did not wear a tie. He jokingly remarked that a He-goat did not need a tie because he naturally had one , referring the long hair throng dangling from the lower jaw of a real he- goat.

When the He- goat came to hosting tent, two gypsy young women flanked him: one held his right hand and the other held the left hand and the three started dancing. As the He-goat had fatty buttocks bulging out like two big melons, the gypsies began singing:

". Shake your thick end , Shake your thick end! O! He _goat!" the invitees burst into laughing. The He-goat angrily pulled his hands off their hands and shouted to them to go away. The gypsies let him go but they continued dancing!

The He- goat sat on a mattress in the middle of the row of mattresses spread on the floor of the hosting tent. One of his friends put an open handkerchief   in front of the He- goat for collecting money donated to the bridegroom as a gift. The invitees, one after another rose and handed the money to a young man standing in front of the He- goat. He would jot down the names of the persons and the quantity of money against their names. This paper would be given to the bridegroom as a reminder of the persons who gave him the money. The money, on such occasions was deemed a debt to be paid to the donor if he or his or brother got married. In other places. The person receiving the money would shout the name of the person and how muchMoney he paid. "Abu Shiqah , two dinars. May Allah recompense him."It was a custom to consider the money donated at wedding ceremonies as debt that had to be paid. The folklore adage says; ' Everything is a loan and debt even if it were eye tears "

When Hadjis ,s turn came to give money to the He-goat, He gave two dinars to Muhajer to hand them to the young man   receiving money for the He- goat. . Muhajer ran away embarrassing Hadjis .He himself had to give the money wedding present to the He-goat. So he gave five instead of two dinars. He went home but the happiness for the He- goat was an evil to Muhajer. Hadjis started beating the boy with his heavy boots till he left the boyhelpless. It was Rifqa who begged him to stop beating the boy, this time.

In the evening, the He- goat was taken to the room of his bride. He entered the room, but at once Wardeh hurried out of the back door screaming. The owl was the first to hear her screaming as she was their nearest neighbor. She hurried to the place and found the He-goat dragging her into the room. He kicked her into the room through the back door. She fell down to the floor of the room and he began beating Wardeh ! The owl hurried to Safi's house asking them to go to the He-goat's house to save their daughter. But one of the young men   hit her with a shoe violently. She ran away saying:" to hell with you! "

In the morning, the owl went to the He- goat home carrying a wide tray full of breakfast food. She told the He-goat's mother that the breakfast was a present from her to the bride and the bridegroom. She knocked at the door. Then the He -goat opened the door. He was surprised to see the owl carrying the tray on her head. She said; "Good morning.Blessed is your morning O bride groom!" The bride groom said:" it is!" but he swiftly took the tray from her and he hurled the tray with the food unto her face. The tray, having a sharp edge,   cut her left cheek and blood gushed at once. The owl burst into yelling. Safi and his young sons harried to the place. They noticed the blood flowing down her face. She told them the story and she would go to the police station. One of the young men said to her firmly" I swear by God if you walk one step towards the police station, I shall shoot you at once. Safi begged her not to go. But she went out into the main dusty street of the village and shouting loudly; " O, people , the bride groom , the He Goat is impotent! He was not successful! 'Two old women ran to her and dragged her into their house. They were the He– goat's aunts, his mother's sisters. They started beating the owl with their shoes. One of them thrust a shoe in her mouth.

A few days passed –by. One of the three young men went under the cover of darkness at midnight to the owl's house. He had a heavy knob stick with him. The owl was a lonely wicked woman who was an instigator of seditions and afflictions among the villagers. She was an inciter of social disorder, she liked to foster tribulation and discord among people by making up stories that caused discord among them. The young man sneaked into her house and began beating her. He left her helpless. She did not recognize him.

All men whose ages were above fifty in that village were illiterate ;there were few of them who could read or write because they went to the most back ward schools during the Ottoman empire colonization of the Arab world!, Those were not official schools - they were called the Kuttab. The teaching staff consisted of one teacher only, the Shake, or scholar as he was called. He taught the pupils the Arabic alphabet and recitation of the Koran; anyone who graduated from the Kuttab was named Khateeb, a person who could recite the Koran and could read and write Arabic.

CHAPTER SEVEN

The principal of the school noticed that there was not any mosque in the village. The practices of the people were not Islamic practices. They were folklore customs rather than religious actions. He also noticed that there were pro agnostic activists who would disseminate irreligious sacrilege beliefs among the young people of the village. So he acted swiftly and went to the headman's house . He told him that he wanted to meet with him and the members of the village council. The headman thought that the principal wanted him to hold a banquet for the school's staff! He said " with pleasure , you and your staff are welcomed tomorrow evening .' the principal said:: " Please, I don't want any banquets, I prefer to meet you and them exclusively "'

At the night of the next day, the twelve members of the village council met with the principal; he addressed them by saying:" Gentlemen, I wish that you understood me clearly! I have been teaching in several villages, but so far I have not seen any village like yours. The pens protruding out of the overt pockets of your jackets and sweaters reveal to me that you are khateebs. This means that you are educated, and as you know! Life is not materialistic only; there is a spiritual aspect of it, the essence of life is to have a spiritual relation with Allah, your creator. And this core of life is absent from this village! In Ramadan, how do you worship your God? How do you hold the Eid ceremony? If someone dies where do you observe   the funeral prayer? . How do you hold the Friday Prayer?" He continued his speech::

" I strongly urge you to build a mosque for the village; the mosque is as important as the school. , It keeps you close to God . It will preserve you and your children from the extreme agnostic current." An old man at once said:" listen to me and all of you be my witnesses that I offer my lot of land , about three thousand square meters for establishing the mosque and if it were not enough you can take additional area from my piece of land adjoining it."

The next day, the headman sent for a builder and told him to start building a mosque. The builder said that he would start the work at once, but he would not take remuneration. He would devote his wages in the way of God, but he expected the council of the village to provide food and wages of the workers he would employ to build the mosque day by day. The head man agreed that money and food for the men would be provided daily, but he asked the builder to start digging the foundations of the mosque as soon as possible! Many young men volunteered to take part in building up the mosque. They did the work for free.   The mosque was finished in less than four months. The day of inaugurating the mosque was assigned and the governor of the region was invited to cut the ribbon for the inauguration.

The problem of the council of the village was finding a qualified Imam to lead the prayer and educate the people about Islamic principles. This man should be experienced and have adequate knowledge of the principles of leading people in worships like Salat (prayer) to be held five times a day besides the weekly ceremony to be held every Friday.

The principal of the school volunteered to lead the prayer temporarily, he said he would lead the prayers at dawn and the afternoon, the evening and the late evening prayers, but he would not be able to lead the noon prayer because he would be at work. The headman said that he or any other khateeb available at that time would lead the noon prayer! This arrangement would last until village council were able to assign a qualified leader (Imam)Two months had passed when the council found an imam for the mosque.

Awwad was the name of the Imam , but he was dubbed Abu Hutheifa. He came from a nearby hamlet. He was qualified; he had an intermediate diploma in religion education.

On Friday, the Imam of the Mosque delivered a speech on the importance of trust in God.

He said that human beings as creatures should submit themselves to the laws of God and they should depend on Him. He reminded the audience that dependence on God entails taking the causes into consideration first. He gave an example of an Arab who lost his she- camel. He said to the prophet, peace be upon, him, that he depended on God to keep his camel for him but the camel went astray and was not able to find it.. The prophet said that you should have tied it and then depended on God, Tie it first ", then depend on God!" He reminded the audience of another tradition on trusting God that stated:" if you truly depend on God , he shall provide you with sustenance and lively- hood as He provides the birds- they leave their nests in the early morning and they come back full." The Imam stressed the verb they **leave** early   and explained that the birds to get their food, they have to look for it through leaving their nests."

He also reminded them of zakat, a certain fixed proportion of the wealth and of each and every property liable to zakat of a Muslim to be paid yearly for the benefit the poor in the Muslim community. The paying of Zakat is obligatory, as it is one of the five pillars of Islam. Zakat is the major economic means for establishing social justice and leading the Muslim society to prosperity and security.

The audience celebrated well the Imam's speech. And it created discussions   among them. Deedis was not happy to see that the villagers highly appreciated the speeches of the Imam and began raising questions such as " look at the water jug on the ground , I want to drink. Let God hand it over to me." Deedis did not believe the Imam . He thought that he should stand against him lest the imam turn the minds of the villagers and if so they would be fatalists.

Some people laughed and went to the Imam to find out the answer. The Imam said:" First of all, we are the slaves of God. He is the Lord, are we the lords or is He the lord? Who created us and created the rules that control the universe. If God had not created hands for us, he would have provided us with the tools necessary for our life. The person asking such a question should ask himself: Hasn't God created arms and hands for him? Why does not he take   the jug with his hand and trust God that he will Quench his thirst with water? Can he ensure that the water will quench his thirst if God does not will?"

Moreover, the Imam said to the audience, the majority of them were teenagers;" Allah is our Lord, but He is different from earthy lords. The lords in earth benefit from their servants; the servants serve their earthy masters. But God carry out everything for you. He provides you with the necessities of life like water and oxygen. Imagine the lack of air, water, and oxygen. There is no meddlers between you and God, you can meet Him at any time you wish, you do not have to follow rules or have appointment; you can address him at any time you like, you can meet and talk to him any time you like! You can beseech him. It is you that schedule your meetings with him as you like! He is Merciful. But you should believe in Him you should fear Him because He watches you all the time, but fearing God is different from fearing His creatures. If you see a lion eager to attack you, you fear it and run away, but if you fear God, you don't flee or runway from Him . You resort to him you hurry to him for protection"

Deedis was very worried to see that the Imam was going to control the village community and he was afraid that were going to be distracted from believing the progressive movement of which he was a member. Therefore, he began instigating people against the Imam; first he said to group of teenagers, Muhjaer among them, that they should not call him Imam. He was just a khateeb, he is not a qualified imam .At this point, Muhajer , asked: "what do you call a person leading people in the Salat?" Deedis answered: " we call him Imam!" Muhajer commented : Then, Shake Awwad is an Imam. Deedis angrily said :" how many a time did I say to you not discuss anything with me, you son of the accursed parents. You are like a noxious thorn in my throat, spoiling everything for me. I will tell your father and let him discipline you!"

. Deedis did not like the existence of the Imam in the village. Therefore, he started attracting teen agers and he fostered his thoughts among them. He taught them that religion is the opium of people!' It kills their thinking process and turns them into fatalists. He would raise questions that they had never heard before like: " the Muslim say that Satan is everywhere; he runs in our veins like blood does, how powerful this creature?   He is poor, he is blamed for every mistake or sin we do!"

Muhajer who was almost fourteen years old commented: "Uncle do you have a radio set? In addition, he asked the other five boys sitting there he same question.They said that they had.Then how many radio sets are there throughout the World? They said that they were countless. One of the boys asked:" what does your question have to do with what Uncle Deedis says?". Muhajer said :" you hear the same program by tuning your radio sets to the station airing it ; you hear it on all the radios at a time! If human beings were able to create such devices that transmit one thing all over the world at a time. Then what about the creation of God who is the Omnipotent, the All -

knowing! They answered "yes", Deedis was astonished and he angrily said: "listen, you son of the perished , never attend a meeting with us! Rise! Get up! Get the hell out of here!, you will thwart all my efforts if you stay with us!" Then, he advised the boys not to listen to him lest he should spoil their minds!

In the evening, Deedis met Hadjis and told him to discipline Muhajer who always thrust his nose in everything . Hadjis went home and as he saw Muhajer, he whipped him severely saying to him:" Never go with the boys to Deedis's meetings! Never comment on whatever he says, Deedis is older than you are. He is a mature man; he is not an underage like you. " Muhajer promised not go to Deedis and he would never talk to him . But he decided to stand firmly against him. He decided to attract the boys to the Imam seminars in the mosque.

Punished by Hadjis , Muhajer sneaked out of home and hurried to the mosque before the evening prayer. He found the Imam there. He told him that his father had punished him because Deedis urged him to do so. The Imam said that he already had heard that Deedis was not pleased with him and he asked the boys not to listen the Imam. Some of the boys told him what happened in the afternoon. He promised Muhajer that he would talk to Hadjis to treat him kindly!

The headman, the school principal, four of the teachers along with a multitude of the villagers attended the evening prayer. Hadjis with his two sons, Faruq and Muhjaer were among them. After the prayer was over, the Imam announced that he would give regular lectures on Islamic education before the evening prayer every Sunday, Tuesday and Thursday. He wished that the fathers of the boys attended with their children such lectures. The headman, the principal and two of the teachers volunteered to help the Imam organize the sessions and take care of the audience that would attend the lectures. The principal said that he would arrange the enrollment of thirty students of the school in those courses. Muhajer happily said that he liked to be one of the students attending the sessions. The principal said: "yes! You `will take care of the attendance log. I will give it you and you would take the roll every session.

Deedis was very vexed at heart, but outwardly he showed off compliance and he did not say anything. He maliciously leered his eyes at Muhjaer when the principal said that he would involve Muhajer with the attendance. After the prayer people went home. The Imam took Hadjis aside and said to him that he was pleased with him and his two sons who observe the prayers regularly. He told him that he admired the smartness of Muhajer and asked him to treat Muhajer kindly so that he would have a self- confident personality in the future. He advised him to foster self confidence in the boy!

That night Thayyar was not able to sleep. So he decided to get rid of Imam. He took his rifle and went at midnight to the Imam's house which was the basement of the mosque. He found the back window open. He fired three bullets through it breaking some jugs and glasses. It was the kitchen. He ran away. So the Imam, hurried to the minaret and began calling for prayer. The villagers were astonished and they hurried to the mosque. They asked him why he was calling for prayer at that time. He showed the headman the traces of the bullets and the broken glasses. The headman sent two young men to the police station for the commander of the police station who came to the scene at once. He said that he would investigate the matter. In the morning the Imam went to the police station and filed an official complaint.The police station was connected with fixed line to the police main office in the center of the region there.

The police commander ordered two of his men to stay at the scene and take care that nobody should come near the scene. In three hours, a land rover with four police officers arrived. There was a huge dog with them. They took him to the Imam's house and they made the dog sniff the traces of the culprit. The dog went directly to Deedis's house. The police did not find him there. He had run away towards the woods near Wazeer Hamlet. As of that time, he was not seen in n the village, as he was wanted for the police. The commander asked the Imam if Deedis had ever tried to make troubles to him. The Imam said that some boys told him that Deedis used to instigate them against him,. The commander summoned the boys and took their affidavits.

Muhajer was perplexed by Deedis's hostile attitude towards the Imam. Before the imam arrived at the village, the majority of the inhabitants used to take his advice about issues related to their familial problems. But when the Imam settled in the village, the villagers overlooked Deedis and trusted the Imam more. They no longer consulted with Deedis or sought his opinion .

Muhajer , the little boy could not absorb what was going around him in that environment ; new terms and words began to creep into his mind: the pastime. Imperialism, Arab nations ; progressive and regressive regions . He was fascinated by to subjects: history and geography; he liked both because the topics were easier to understand. He liked to scrutinize the maps and memorize the names of the capitals of the countries. He was also pleased to know that the Arabs are too many to be defeated by any external force! He memorized an ode:

Arab countries are my homes
From Damascus to Baghdany
From Najd to Yemen ,
to Egypt and Tattwan
Neither a border nor a religion
segregate us
The tongue of dhadh (Arabic language)
ties us to Ghassan and Adnan(the Arabs forefathers)
We had a past civilization
We shall revitalize it and we shall dig it up
Even if it were buried,

We shall do that even if all
The cunning rallied against us.
So come on, children of my nation,
 Ascend the heights through knowledge
 And sing, my mother's children,
The Arab countries are my homes!"

The principal once heard Muhajer chanting that song loudly in the yard of the school. He summoned him to his office. He asked Muhjaer: "Why were you chanting the song loudly?"

Muhajer said:" I like this song very much!"

The principal said :" you have disturbed the classes by singing loudly.' Never do that again you're one the best students at school. I don't expect you to do that again.' A teacher remarked: '"This boy is poor; he does not know the reality. Once I was going to visit my sister in an Arab country: I had to wait for three months to get a visa ,and when I arrived the border check point, I had to spend three days in the open till they let me enter their country. Sing, my son, sing! Arab countries are my homes! The future is ahead of you!"

The term 'regressive' was difficult for Muhjer to absorb its meaning. He thought that anyone who is older than him could explain it to him. He often heard the elderly say:" The one who is a day older than you has a year of knowledge more than you do!"

So he asked a shepherd of thirty years old who was standing at Dhughayyem's house front yard; He asked him; "uncle! Can you tell me the meaning of ' regressive'?" The shepherd was pleased to hear the question so he tried to explain the meaning of regressive to Muhajer. Holding a stick horizontally at both ends with his hands, the shepherd walked backward without looking behind himself; he said to the boy: "Look at me while I am going regressively .while I am facing you! The boy shouted to him: "Look out! Look out! There is a pit behind you!" It was a deep hole dug in the front yard of the house. But it was too late; the shepherd fell with his heavy weight down the deep pit. The boy began shouting;" help! Help!" A few men hurried to the deep pit and used a pulley wheel to drag the shepherd out of the deep pit. Muhajer asked himself: "Are the   regressive countries going to fall in deep pits like the shepherd?",

People began to feel insecure because the village was at the frontline. Muhajer would feel secure, because he knew that his father and Uncle Dhughayyem were armed with effective rifles. Moreover, his father and about fifteen men would go every night and guard the village for the night. The presence of village guards reinforced his sense of security. It was impossible for any intruders to infiltrate the village while those valiant guards with their rifles in their hands! Some of the guards would often sing:

> We are the terror to the enemy,
> Seeking a debt to be paid,
> Injustice is never accepted by any men
> Except those whose mother's brothers are ignoble!
> Listen, O, usurper of our right.
> One day we shall attain it
> Then we would march towards the aggressor
> Who betrayed the covenant and religion?
> And we shall hold them accountable
> For their actions

Despite his feeling of security, Muhajer always thought of the complex sources of insecurity. These sources were the teachers (like Anter) at school, the parents at home   the police station and Deedis and the enemy beyond the front line.

Hadjis built a house on his farm. It was near a dusty track running along a water gutter   that passes by his land. Beyond the house, there was a plenty of arable land. Once he planted the land with watermelon plants. When the plants of the watermelon had fully grown, their branches crept long on the ground .and they produced great quantity of watermelons that some of them were too heavy for Muhajer to carry. . One day Qassimand Muhajer's cousin, who was five years older than he was, went to the melon field of Qassim's father. The melons were big and Qassim wanted   to break one of them for Muhjaer to eat.

Before breaking the water melon fruit , Qassim tested it with a small knife; he took a small slice out of it to see whether it was ripened   enough to be eaten. The red color of the core of the watermelon would indicate whether it was ripened or not.

One day Mujaher went into his father's watermelon field. There were many big melons; he wanted to check whether they were ripened or not. He marked seven big melons with his penknife, but he hid the marking spot by overturning the melon with the broken rind touching the soil. The melons were heavy; they would not move by the wind. A week later Hadjis checked his melons. To his surprise, he saw about seven melons withering with yellow rind! When he turned them over, he discovered that they had been marked with a knife. He thought that it was Qassim who spoiled his melons. He had seen him passing by the field one day.

Two days later, Haleemah, Hadis's daughter was going to see her grandmother in the village which was far from Hadjis 's house. Muhajer quarreled with her and he prevented her by hitting her. Qassim hurried to them and violently hit Muhajer at the back of his head with his right fist. The boy fell down to the dusty road; his mouth was full of grains of soil; he began crying. Hadjis came running, but Qassim had left and started running lest Hadjis catch him. Hadjis went directly to Dhughayyem's house. He found Qassim sitting there quietly by his father near the coffee fire. Hadjis sat down and had some coffee! Then he addressed Qassim:" Why did you hit Muhjaer? You broke his head with your fist. You had done something else. There are seven big melons of mine marked by a small knife. Nobody had such a knife except you. I saw you the other day passing by my field. For sure, you did it." Dhughayyem got very angry and instantly hit Qassim with the pounding wooden hand of the coffee pestle, breaking his right arm !

A week later, Hadjis noticed that Muhajer had a penknife with him. So, he asked him:" why did you mark the seven melons?" The boy was taken aback He timidly said:" I saw Qassim marking his father's melons, so I tried to see whether our melons were ripen enough." Hadjis got strained and angry.

He regretted the harm he caused to Qassim. So he began kicking the boy with his right leg! While he was kicking the boy, he saw a very huge dark brown stallion racing through his crop of melons. The horse was running very fast breaking the biggest melons in the field. There was a diagonal raw of broken red melons- they were much ripened. The field was strewn with red chain of broken red melons. Hadjis went running to his crops; there were forty-nine broken melons. They were utterly destroyed by the sturdy hooves of the stallion! He said: "we are for God and unto Him we shall return! Justice has prevailed. Muhjaer wrongly hit Haleema ; he was punished by Qassim ,who hit Mujaher, but he had his hand broken by Dhughayyem. I accused Qassim of marking the melons when he was innocent. Now God sent this horse to punish me. I lost 49 melons for wronging Qassim. God forgive me! We are for God and unto Him we shall return. He realized that justice shall always prevail!

In the afternoon the headman and the owner of the stallion came to Hadjis . They sat in the   shade of a cinchona tree. The owner of the stallion offered Jababr a hundred dinars as compensation for the destroyed melons. Hadjis refused to take the money. The owner of the horse insisted. Hadjis took the money and handed it to the headman asking him to give to the Mosque charity committee who were raising money for the poor. The headman thanked him. Hadjis told them that Go sent the stallion to teach him that justice 'shall always prevail even if people were unmindful of it.'
The mosque stirred a new style of life in the village, an active dynamic style of social life especially on Fridays. Friday was supposed to be a holiday, but for the village it became a busy day! The village became a beehive; on Friday. People would pour into the village from all directions. They would travel journeys near and far! People would gather at the mosque to observe the Friday prayer ceremony, but the most majestic sight was that of the military trucks and land rovers that would come in convoys transporting the soldiers to observe the prayer. Children, women and young men would feel proud of the soldiers who were dressed in full military uniform with glittering buttons and emblems of the Army stuck in their berets over their forefronts. The mosque would be crowded with soldiers and people from outside the village as well as the natives. When the mosque was too crowded, the inhabitants would pray in the yard. The mosque would take 500 individuals but the crowd attending the Friday prayer   were more than a thousand person so the yard of the mosque was utilized for prayer. ,

Observing prayer times, the inhabitants of the became keen to evalute time.. They began to sense the importance of time. Prayer must be performed in time because there is a warning in the Quran   to those who are unmindful of their prayer:" In chapter 108 : " woe unto to those performers of Salat(prayers)) . Those who are unmindful of their Salat (prayers) asthey don't observe   their stated fixed times)." The best prayer is the Salat performed in its fixed time.

Before the establishment of the mosque, people would not care about time, but now they had to observe the times of prayer. Moreover, prayer entailed the individual be clean body and soul. Muslims must do the ablution five times a day at the times of prayer. Because they have to observe the individual or the congregation prayers. They have to clean their private parts, their hands, faces, arms and feet besides wiping their heads with wet hands . It is advisable to use the midway (wooden tooth brush) to clean their teeth before performing the prayer. Some people were surprised when the Imam told them that they had to enter the bathroom with their left foot first and they started to laugh. But, they were surprised that they have to observe more fifteen conditions upon entering the W.C .Realizing the astonishment of some people who showed their mockery and sarcasm of entering the bathroom with the left foot, the Imam said:" Entering the bath room with left foot first   is one condition, but there are other fifteen conditions to be observed when you enter the bathroom. This means that Islam is a religion of discipline; it regulates all the affairs of a Muslim life especially keeping himself clean, spiritually, and physically. It implants self-confidence in him. It preserves the mind of the individual. Third of the Quran urges the individuals to use their

Minds. The Quran urges human beings to think and contemplate the Imam reminded the audience that soldiers when they march in training or parades move their left feet first. Muslims should not be parrots or blind imitators. You must realize that God does endow us with minds but he does not set laws against them.

Muslims have to look deep into things; they should observe the teachings of their religion that organize their lives and   discipline them and they have to live in harmony with the environment around them, with itsliving beings. Not only humans, but also the animals and plants or the earth itself. They should treat the animals kindly ,The Imam reminded them of a tradition about the man who was rewarded with heaven : The man was very thirsty , he was walking through a desert .Then he came to a well, he went down and drank some water, when the man came out of the well he saw a thirsty dog panting. So he said to himself "The dog is very thirsty as I had been." He went down the well and filled his shoe with water and held it with his teeth as he was climbing up the ladder of the well and gave the dog the water to drink!

The Imam noticed that the boys of the village would take the birds young out of their nest   making the mothers of the small birds unhappy. He urged parents to stop this practice. He asked them: "Do you like that other people kick you out of your houses and take your children, slaughter them in front of your eyes and fry them in a frying pan? How would you feel if this happened? He reminded them of a tradition telling the story of the sky lark whose young were taken by one of the prophet's companions and the terrified skylark came flapping its wings above the army. The prophet, peace upon Him asked;' who bereaved the sky lark with its young?   He ordered the man who took its young to return them to their nest.

Muhajer encouraged his class mates not to rob the nests of the sparrows at their homes. The following year most of the nests were left intact_no body dared to terrify the birds by taking their young out of their nests.

The Imam emphasized that animals ' have sentiments and instincts like human beings!" He told them a story about a snake which was about two meters long. Its hole was near a Bedouin black tent. It had a nest with her young. One morning the man saw the snake leaving its nest leaving her young in the nest. He decided to take her young and keep them away. He wanted to check the snake's reaction when she did not find her young. When the snake came back, she did not find her young in the nest. Therefore, she went to the man's water jar and she began ejecting her poison into the water Jar. Then she left quickly. She wanted to avenge herself by poisoning the water of the man and his family. Thinking it was the man or one of his family members who took away her young. When the snake was away from her nest, the man returned the snake's young to the nest. When the snake came back to her nest, she found her young intact in the nest. She quickly encircled the water jar and turned it down. The water flew out of the jar. The Imam, told the audience to consider the animals as living creatures with instinctive recognition and if they were treated kindly, they treat you kindly!

The villager's attitude was positively modified towards the treatment of animals. They began to realize that animals though they cannot verbally express themselves, their behavior manifest that they have feelings and sentiments like human beings.

One day an ill old man came riding his horse to see the doctor at the clinic of the village. While he was tying the horse to a tree, the horse started beating the ground with her forelegs and neighing at the same time. The horse looked terrified. A crowd of people hurried to her. To their surprise, they saw the owner of the horse dead and there were tears flowing out of the horse's eyes! It is well known that the genuine Arabian horses are the most loyal friends to their owners!

He reminded them of the public adage that stated: "the good word brings the snake out of its hole!"

He also advised them against confining cats, he reminded them of the prophet's tradition stating that a woman entered hell, because she confined a cat and prevented it from fending for itself.

The most remarkable thing brought about was the sanitation of the village. The garbage of the houses used to be thrown outside the houses in the streets and the lanes of the village. The Imam told the inhabitants that "their faith is incomplete if they throw the garbage in the lanes and pollute the springs of water and the atmosphere by burning the garbage in front of the houses.

The principal of the school and the Imam of the mosque would hold sessions for educating the Muslims of the principles of Islam. Many teen-agers would go to those sessions. Meanwhile, old women with a few men were not pleased with the activities of the Imam and the principal. Deedis of and a few of the so-called Khateebs , were not pleased with the new situation: Deedis believed that the people of the of the village , if the imam were not stopped , would be fatalists. Deedis returned home after the Imam withdrew his complaint against him. The commander of the police station had him sign a warranty not to hurt the Imam.. Though Deedis signed a warranty not use force against the Imam, he resorted to passive resistance.

Deedis resorted to a sorcerer, Shake Karandas who used to sell amulets to women especially the old ones who would hang those amulets in their homes for protection. Karandas would instigate those women who came to him asking them not to accept what the Imam of the mosque tried to convince people of!

Karandas and Deedis were the ringleaders that carried out a propaganda campaign against the Imam! Among their followers was the He-goat. He was an irresponsible person. He was impulsive in his actions. He would do things without thinking about them first. But, 'He who digs a bit for his brother will fall therein!) Karandas was contriving to eradicate the Imam and the school principal from the village, he himself was eradicated by his own actions.

Prior to the Friday ceremony, the Imam gave a lecture about those who deceive the poor people, especially old women and take their money saying: "They are magicians and sorcerers who trick people!" Deedis and Karandas were present, so Deedis called out : " Shake Karandas , you are invited to have dinner with me tonight at my tent." The Imam said that a Muslim should put his trust in God, and he will be successful in his life.

Deedis commented: " You are a fatalist , Imam , you say if I put my trust in God ,he would facilitate my actions to be successful. I do believe in experiment only, now, look, I am taking the pen out of my pocket. Now I am putting it on the ground. I put my trust in your God, let Him pick the pen and give it to me."

The Imam thought for a moment, then he said; "what a big mind you have! As you do believe in experiment, we will do another experiment now.   The imam rose up and went to a cabinet in the corner of the mosque, he fetched a box of Turkish delight, uncovered it and asked the people there to take one piece each. When Deedis was about to pick one, the Imam said: "stop! Wait a minute , with what are you going to pick the piece?" Deedis answered :" with my fingers." The imam said: ' The experiment now begins . I will wrap your fingers with this piece of cloth so that you cannot use them.   The imam wrapped the fingers of Deedis's right hand and asked him to pick one piece, but Deedis failed. The imam said:" you see, you failed to pick a piece of the Turkish delight because your fingers were tied. Now, I will release them and set them free. Pick the piece!" Deedis picked the piece. The Imam asked: "how did you get your hand? Who created it for you? Can you create one?" Deedis was embarrassed thinking that the Imam was not going to give him a piece of the Turkish delight. He said: "How come, you are a wise man and you think that God will pick it up for me? You believe in God and you say that He is the Lord of the worlds and you think he will come and pick a piece of a Turkish delight for me!"
The Imam said : Allah is the greatest: now you have answered yourself. How do you say that Allah is your Lord and you are his slave   when you wanted Him to be your servant? Moreover, He has created for you the organs you need in life. . Can you pick the Turkish delightwithout using your fingers? Can you walk without legs and feet? Can you see without eyes? Who provided you with these organs? Be sure that if He had not provided you with hands He would have subjected other creatures to serve you. Let me tell you an authentic story:
Thirty years ago I went to my father to see him at the hay stack after he had threshed the wheat stalks, he separated the grains from chaff ; he heaped the grain on the ground waitingfor me to help him take the grains home. It was late in the afternoon when I noticed a rock lizard coming to the heap of wheat. It filled its mouth with wheat grains and went away running. The lizard did this several times. It aroused my curiosity. Then, I followed it .When   it came to take the grains. I

traced its track. It was an incredible sight: Why do you think the lizard was taking the grain? I was very surprised to see it with my naked eye. There was a blind skylark settling in its nest and it opened its mouth for the lizard to pour the grains of wheat there in.? This event I saw by myself, can you tell me who subjected the lizard to the sky lark?. God created the essential organs for you, can you live properly without a brain? Imagine that you lost an organ of your five senses .how life would be for you. Deedis commented that the incident was theoretical you cannot prove it." The Imam said   ; Come with me tomorrow at sun set before it gets dark to the huge rocks at the foot of the mount to the west of the village. I will show you something similar to that case."

Before sun set, Deedis and the Imam went to the huge rock. In the shade of that, rock was an owl. They both sat at two huge rocks about fifty meters away of the owl. The Imam told Deedis not make any noise and not bother the owl. The owl was perching there hooting. Fifteen minutes later she stopped hooting.A robin flew from one rock to another and landed directly between the feet of the owl. The owl immediately helped itself on the bird and began eating it. The Imam said: "Have you seen what happened. I heard about this from old people. You saw how the owl gets food every night. Tomorrow the scene will be repeated with another robin! You can come and see it". Deedis said:" Tomorrow, I will prove to you that this scene will not occur again."Deedis thought of another perplexing question: ' he said:" what is the fault of the robin to be eaten by a worthless owl?"

The Imam said: first of all Allah cannot be questioned as to what he does , but human beings can be ! All creation is not created haphazardly , every creature has task to accomplish.

The next day after the late evening prayer, Deedis went to headman's hosting house where the majority of the village men were meeting. He was carrying a leather bag with him. He sat by the Imam. The Imam asked:" Did you go there?"

Deedis said happily:" Yes, I went there and I told you that the owl would not eat any robins anymore!"

The Imam said; " I agree with you . The dead don't eat."

Deedis said; "how do you mean?'

The Imam said: "Have you ever seen a dead person eating? The owl cannot eat now,   because you killed it with your rifle, and it is in your bag . Take it out, come on!"

Puzzled, Deedis asked: "Do you know the unseen! How did you know that I killed it?"

The Imam said:" A genie told me! He saw you and told me!" the people present burst into laughing."

The Imam said: "listen Deeds! I don't know the unseen, but by this action you proved that you are agnostic and have materialistic foundations of your thought. You resorted to violence when you fail to convince others of your thought. You often try to erase the facts that contradict your belief. But you forgot if there were only one owl in the valley, you would be mistaken, because there are many owls there. The majority of the people here may have witnessed an owl preying on a small bird that came it without any effort exerted by the owl to catch it. You saw yesterday the robin when it came to the owl by itself! I do not know the unseen. I had no spirit to tell me your news. In fact, it was Muhajer who saw you shoot the owl and he came and told me, begging me to advice you against killing innocent birds like the owl! The boy likes these birds!" you know he was born in a hamlet among the hills abounding with owls. And he used to hear them hooting at night.

In the evening of the next day Karandas went to   have dinner at at Deedis's tent, Deedis's neighbor , a black man in his fifties, whose two daughters were black , asked one of them to help Deedis's wife prepare dinner. After the meal Karandas had to wash his hands. The black girl who was, seventeen, hurried and held a kettle of water .She went with Karandas a few meters away from the ten She began pouring water on Karandas's hands. . Then, Karandas whispered to her :""The black color goes well with the white one.!. I think they match properly!" The girl laughed timidly and said; "yes, you are right, see you tomorrow at your cavern."

According to the customs prevailing the rural   society , anyone who attended a banquet and eats there , should invite the guest and the persons present to have food at his home!   An adage was: "Food of men is debt for men, but for rascals, it is charity!"So , Murashad the black man , insisted that Karandas have dinner with him and Deedis tomorrow night. Deedis said that he would not able to attend the banquet , because it was his turn to observe the night watch of the village .Hadjis excused himself but sent Muhajer to help Murashad. Muhajer hurried to help Karandas , but the latter   pushed him away saying that he would not let him help him. So Muhajer got angry and left for his home. Karandas did not like Muhajer because he thought he was a follower of the Imam!

Seeing Karands push the boy away, the black girl carried the kettle to pour water for Karandas to wash his hands. When she approached him in the darkness he tried to grab her breast ! The girl shouted in terror; her father hurried with his heavy knob stick and beat rapidly and successively him with a heavy knobstick. Karandas started crying, but Murashad continued beating him. Murashad , then,   asked his daughter to hand him , the bamboo cane and he hit him eighty times on his fatty buttocks and his leg calves!

Karandas had some of his ribs broken and he had a lot of bruises all over his body; he could hardly move: he shouted: "For God's sake feel pity on me!" he begged Murashad !

Murashad said : " listen , you devil, I thought that there was a pious scholar under your turban ! But it turned out it was the devil himself there! Now let us have a deal! If want to stay here in this village I will let the cat out of the bag! And I will let people around know your reality, but if you want to leave the village for good, I can help you!"

Karandas said that he would like to go to Jerusalem region and he would wait until tomorrow morning . Murashad said. " BY God , you shall not sleep this night at this village !

Waiving   the bamboo stick in hi right hand , Murahadasked   karandas howmuch money he earnedthrogh swindling the old women of th village. Karandas said that he had little money   but Murashed rsuemd beating him. Karandas begegd to stop and he pe would give him all the money he had taken romthe old woman, it was about 500 Jd , afortune at that time. MUrashed asked him to give teh names of the old woman whom he had swindled. It turned out that almost all the old women had visited the cavern and had been swindled several times by Karandas Murashad said:" You have to leave now!" So he went with Murashad to the cavern , his dwelling . he took some yellow books and papers. Taking the money from Karands ,   Murashad carried him on his donkey, and took him to the

Jordan river   they crossed the river through a shallow ford and
Murashed left him on the high way to Jerusalem! Where he took
a bus to Jerusalem. No news was heard about him since then!

Before noon Murashad told Deedis what happened . he said that he had taken money from him and he wanted to give it the Imam as charity. Deedis was startled . He said: " you are insane. This an opportunity for us to gain the confidence of the villagers, we shall use the money to gain the confidence of propel. The imam has been destroying their minds ." two nights later deedis sent two men of his group and they threatened Murashed,robing him of the money he had taken from Karandas.

A week later, some young men went into Karandas's cavern and brought a considerable quantity of angular amulets, pieces of paper with a list of the old women who used to ask for the amulets! The owl had been the most frequent visitor to Karanads as the papers show. She had asked him to give her discord spells for almost all the families of the village.

When the boys opened the amulets they found that they all carried the same spell: 'Iqra Karandas ; kuf wa- ehbis! That is, O, Karandas read , ward off and imprison!"

After , Karandas's departure another sorcerer came to the village but he was kicked out of it at once. The villagers had learnt the lesson well-there would be no place for a sorcerer, a hypocrite liar among them. Therefore, soothsayers had departed from the village forever!

Corporal punishment was a normal practice at schools during those days. Parents would not object to such practice as long as it is in the interest of the education process though some teachers were ruthless. One day a student, a trouble- maker was sent to the school administration office; the teacher noticed that his palms were smeared with blood. Both palms were almost covered with blood, When the principal asked the students for the reason he answered that he had killed a rock brown lizard and dyed his palms with its blood to harden the skin of his palms to withstand the   corporal punishment with the canes of the teachers.

In the fall of 1966 , a great offensive was launched by Israel   on a small village in Hebron region. Many civilians were killed and there were several raids on the front line villages in the West bank and the East bank of Jordan.

Demonstrations overwhelmed Jordan: crowds were into the streets in marches and demonstrations in all the cities. The demonstrations were instigated by The Arab voice of Egypt and some underground pro -Arab activists like Deedis and the likes. Demonstrations continued till the war broke out on June ,5 , 1967 .

Demonstrations and turbulences led to the closure of the schools throughout the country. Streets were closed. The routine of the daily life was interrupted and the general atmosphere was charged with tension. Farmers were not able to export their products to the main markets of the country.

These incidents were backed up by the pan Arab radios broadcasting chants and songs urging people to topple down the regime in Jordan and other Arab countries. "Bats of the night" and ' sand snakes' manipulated those incidents for their benefits. , but the government acted swiftly and deployed more of the police forces in the main cities and villages around them. Deedis with a dozen of young men marched through the dusty lanes of the village chanting some of the songs aired by the Arab voice Radio . When they got to the water spring they stopped under the shade of the a huge Sidra (lote tree). There, Deedis enthusiastically shouted: ; " soon we shall recover all of our usurped land thanks to the struggle of the grand leader , our great leader. The leader of the Arab nation.

In May 1967, the students of the school which was not far from the police station noticed that the horse men force mounted their horses and left the place at once. Meanwhile, a force of eight camel men arrived with their camels at the station. The uniform of those men was remarkable. It was like an Arab cloak with red bandoleers crossing the chest and a silver dagger protruding from the soldier's belt.

Rumors were circulated throughout the village: The camel police men were ruthless; anyone taking part in a demonstrations ,if he happened to fall in their hands,   , the soldiers like wolves would tear his neck with their teeth! .

The headman of the village did not go to the police station to welcome the force as he used to do when new personnel arrived at the station. The lanes were quite at night; it was a ghost village. Before the arrival of the camel force, the boys of the village would stay for almost the whole night in the lanes during the moonlit nights. Now, with the presence of this terrifying force, silence and tranquility weighed down on the whole village even the dogs were silent at night.   Everything seemed terrified even the frogs of the ponds would not croak at night.

On a Thursday, Qassim, son of Dhughayyem , came riding his donkey to buy some groceries and take them home to his father's tent which was pitched beyond remote hills about eight miles to the south of the village , He dropped by at Hadjis's house and begged his uncle to let Muhajer and Faruq go with him to spend the week end with him at their uncle's home. The boys went and spent the night there,

While they were heading for Dhughayyem's tent ,Qassim told the two boys that there was a kite nest on a high rock in the canyon the they would pass through . It was late in the afternoon when they got to the nest . Qassim , took of his shoes and climbed up the high rock. When he got to the nest, he happily cried:" There are four young birds and he started throwing them to the ground. The birds were not mature enough to fly. So they took them home. The boys arrived Dhughayyem's tent after the sun set . When Dhughayyem saw the young kite birds ,he got very angry and started throwing stones at Qassim. He said angrily;" You cannot make use of these birds, their mother will attack us to-night. Go at once and put them back in their nest." So, Qassim and the two boys went in the darkness, they heard dogs barking. Qassim said they were barking at a hyena. The two boys were terrified and they wanted to go back to their uncle's tent, but Qassim said he was kidding. When they got to the high rock, it was very dark and it was dangerous to climb up the rock in the darkness. Qassim took the young birds one by one, broke their wings, and threw them up the rock into the large nest. The birds were screeching of pain. Then the three boys ran home. They arrived late and Dhughayyem was very angry. He hit Qassim with a shoe.

On Friday sunny morning around ten o'clock Qassim accompanied his two cousins to the old Turkish pools in the valley nearby. There was a rivulet with brackish water running by the old Turkish swimming pools. They swam there for two hours. Then they gathered some dates from the palm trees growing by the rivulet. Finally, they decided to go home.

Qassim advised them to walk along the newly asphalted road leading to the village, hoping that a car may pass by and take them home. The two boys walked for half an hour, but not a car appeared. They were walking along a wide curve between two high hills as they were going along the curve, they heard a car roaring behind them. Suddenly the car appeared; it was a land rover, the driver's cabin was blue and the rear cabin was covered with a canvass cloth. The car stopped, but the boy's faces turned pale with fear as they realized that the men in the car were members of the camel force as they could tell from their uniforms. The driver smiled to them showing his glittering golden tooth. He asked them:" Where are you going?" They said they were going home at Munqatta'a. The driver asked them to get into the back chamber of the vehicle. To their surprise, there was a soldier sitting there, he smiled and happily welcomed them. He offered them some candies and army biscuits! When they got home they asked the driver to stop and let them go, but the soldier in the back chamber gave them a substantial quantity of candies and much biscuit and told them to give his regards to their parents.

On Saturday morning, the two boys Faruq and Muhajer went to school taking with them some of the candies and biscuits. They told the other boys that the camel force men gave them a lift to the village in their land-rover and they offered them some candies and biscuits. They were very gentle and they were generous. They were not as wicked as Deedis and his group alleged. Almost all the village inhabitants heard of the news and life began to permeate the village again.

Hadjis was pleased to know that the camel force men gave a lift to his sons and he thought of honoring them. Hadjis went the headman of the village and he said to him that the village did not receive the camel force properly. Instead, they ignored them and had not any kind of contact with them. They should have invited them according to the Arabian custom that new comers or those who dwell in the area near your home, must be honored by the dwellers of the place: newcomers should be treated as guests. It is an old Arabian tradition that people who share food, bread and salt, become brothers and they never betray one another!

He told him that those camel men were sons of noble tribes and they should be honored by the inhabitants. They should be treated as guests! The headman hesitated saying that would create discord in the village: Deedis and his men were circulating rumors against the camel force: they would say that the hadjjanah(camel force) were ruthless; with their nails and teeth they would treat the necks of their victims. victims with nails and teeth . They were generous enough to give the two boys a lift. Besides giving them candies and biscuits.

Hadjis said,: "If you are afraid of Deedis, I'll invite and honor them at my house! I am going to them now! I know these people well; I know that they are honest! I served in the national guard with tribe men like them: our commander is the brother of one of them."

The headman was bewildered and surprisingly asked: "How did you know that one of them was the brother of your commander?" Hadjis answered:" Yesterday , the one who gave biscuits and candies to my sons, when they passed by the old site of national gurd company he said to the boys that his brother was the commander of that company and he had visited him there. So I realized that he was the brother of my ex-commander!." Hadjis stood up and was about to leave. But the head man said:" wait!   Wait, I'll go with you but you will be responsible for Deedis's reaction".

Hadjis and the headman went to the police station. The commander of the station received them warmly. He was a young man in the late forties. He was dressed in a white dishdashah ,. A corporal welcomed them, offering them some coffee to drink.

The police station was a forte. It was built during the Turkish rule of the Arab land. It was built of boulders of stone. The forte was well fortified and it needed little maintenance. Hadjis and the headman were amazed at the strong walls. The commander remarked : " You look puzzled by these stones , this building was a detention center   like all the other fortes throughout the Livy ; the Ottoman authorities used to detain the young men and concentrate them in those fortes and then send them to the frontlines to fight for the Ottoman empire.

The commander said: "It is true that they had colonized us for more than four hundred years, but those years were the period of long darkness and ignorance: That rule fostered enmity, hatred and wars among tribes. Their long rule of this land yielded two bitter fruits: ignorance and sickness. If you roam the Arab world vast area,   looking for landmarks for scientific progress during that era, you would only come across the detention centers and   fortes. Only ignorance weighed down on the Arab world. Tell me whether your grandfathers educated or not? Did they or their mates go to school , can you find any school buildings around that were built during the Ottoman reign of the area, are there any hospitals?   Mention to me the names of any remarkable scholars, scientists, or physicians like Zahrawi and ibn al Haitham, Kindi al- Razi and Ibn Sina. Were there any Arab scholars or scientists who excelled in astronomy, pure science medicine and other fields of human knowledge? Ask any person of the elderly about the social practices that Ottoman rule fostered among the Arab societies and tribes: it encouraged them to invade one another. Tribe –x would invade tribe –y, they would kill the men, take their camels, sheep or cattle if they had any. If the Ottoman had not ruled the Arab world, The Arabic language would have been the first international language. In 1516 , the Sultan banned the printing press and decreed that anyone who owned a typewriter or a printing press must be sentenced to death. Ask your grandfathers if they are still alive : did they not   pay taxes for a tribehead who was a bidder or ' mulatazim' who was called Shake by the Arabs   but in fact he was a slave for the Turks .History books swarm with forgeries by biased writers

Sects always promote their thought and ideas, they try to forge reality, forgetting that the land they live on. is still there. Don't forget the authenticity of history can be verified by the reality of the land where a certain event took place , for the land constantly proves the authenticity of history or nullifies it. The land is the mother of reality! No matter how eloquent you are or whether you have universal propagandists, or representatives, you cannot forge reality that exists in the land. If you want to make sure of the reality of a historical claim, resort to the land! It will tell you the truth. The land does not tell lies or fabricate history. They said in the past 'our archeological monument testify our reality!" The stones of this castle witness to the authenticity of my argumentation!" then he continued:

"One more point to make: the mobs should not control our lives. Decisions appealing to the mobs wishes and that are taken under the pressure of the mobs will be destructive decision! We should not lend our brains to the mobs to dumb their rubbish in; if we do so we will end in perdition in this life and the life hereafter. Decisions for cheap publicity   will destroy us. War is not a game or a show off. You can judge whatever you hear is credible or not.

The commander concluded that: "Anyway , I am pleased that you at last a showed up and honored us by your presence here!" The headman, then, said that he and the men of his village   would have the honor to invite the   commander and his men to have dinner the day after tomorrow! The commander agreed and the coffee was served.

The next morning was the 4th of June, 1967. A corporal arrived at the headman's guesthouse and told the headman to postpone the banquet to be held   . When asked for the reason, he said that the general atmosphere was not   appropriate for such an occasion especially in the south border(Egypt). The war is looming in the horizon; it may break out at any moment.

In the evening a detachment of soldiers from the nearby garrisons arrived at the village in two Ford lorries and they began digging two trenches for mortars in the plain to the south of the village. They were about thirty to forty meters away from the houses of the village.

CHAPTER Eight

The next day was Monday, the fifth of June 1967. Hadjis was picking the Tomato fruits with the help of his mother , his wife, and the children. It was a hot morning. Around ten o'clock, a tremendous deafening roaring of planes filled the sky. Looking up to the sky, Hadjis saw two aircraft flying from east heading west. They were about two kilo meters away, they were black in color and the glass of the cockpits was glittering, He shouted loudly: "May Allah greet you! They are Iraqi planes!" No sooner did he utter those words, than a series of tremendous explosions and flames devastated the military garrison, which was about two miles away to the south of the village. It was set ablaze! There were successive loud explosions: the planes bombed the site there.

A few minutes later, two artillery shells landed at the deserted site of mortars to the south of the village. The headman and the village council decided to evacuate the village and send the inhabitants to the nearby dales and valleys of the hilly area to the south west of the village. A few minutes later, hundreds of women, old men and children were hurrying on foot, or riding donkeys with some of their effects carried on the donkeys. Many children were screaming and trembling of terror!

Hadjis decided to go back to his cavern in the grove but the unexpected happened. That was on the second day of the war, the slopes of the mountains with the heath of dry flora were burnt as the Israelis set fire to the area by shelling the western highest peak of the largest mountain and fire was set to the dry grass. The high grass was slanted to the east by the west wind and the fire went raging with the speed of the wind blowing from the west. The whole mountains were set ablaze. People started to go back to the village. When they got home, they did not believe what they saw. Their homes were robbed by their fellow Arabs: the enemy had not arrived yet. The groceries were emptied and even some of them were burnt.

An old woman had her arm and leg broken when she tried to resist a shepherd: she shouted to him: "You were a friend! Why are you robbing my home?" He shouted to her: "To hell with you! Go away, old woman of evil." and he with a hard wood mallet hit her arm and leg violently breaking both! . Moreover, he set fire to the house leaving it in flames!

When the old woman asked for the reason behind the shepherd behavior, he said :

"Listen! You old woman of evil; May Allah curse your gray hair, don't ask me why! You seem to ignore your bad treatment of me when you employed me as a cowboy for you for more than ten years taking care of your cattle! "He added, ;" when you got your son married, you sang those humiliating songs , they were so degrading not only to me but to all the refugees like me .I have been filled up with spite and I have been eager to punish you for your maltreatment of me since that event when you sang:

By Allah I will sell a refugee for a crust of bread !

Can't you remember when you said to your donkey:" gee , gee! Your face looks like the face of a refugee! May Allah curse you, O, Refugees! They knocked on a tin for you and you fled your homes." He added: " Do you remember when you refused to let your son marry your niece, because she was a refugee?" He continued;" Now, it's your time to become a refugee! You should know that time is perfidious! Times change! Accursed may be your grey hair. Go to hell."

A few minutes later, there was aloud shout: "O people run away . Run away! Go away, take your women with you. If they stay here, they will be raped!"

Groups of people were fleeing their houses from the nearby villages and were heading for the east. All the people of the village were terrified to hear the word 'rape'. To preserve their honor and dignity, they had to keep their women immune to raping and the only way to keep them so was to flee with the multitudes of people pouring to the east.

Panic overwhelmed the whole village. Multitudes of people fleeing their houses from the frontlines villages were hurrying to the east. Some people were walking, others were riding donkeys or horses. People were scattered like moths throughout the plains around the village! They were fleeing in disorder.

Sablud held his white scarf (a surrendering sign) high on a long stick in both hands when he heard an aircraft high in the sky. It was emitting   two lines of white smoke. It was so high that it looked like a glittering bird with   white jets of smoke after it!

The mobs were spreading terrifying stories about the atrocities committed by the invaders. The mobs aggravated the state of terror among the people and speeded up the fleeing of the inhabitants out of the region: They fled for safer places; The mobs thought that they were doing the right thing for the inhabitants They thought that by spreading rumors they would protect the inhabitants from the atrocities of enemy. The inhabitants were in isolation from the rest of world, the only contact with the outer world was through the Arab Voice Radio   transmitting hoaxes about defeating the enemy!

Along a dusty track to the East of the Jordan river, there were multitudes of women, children and men moving up the high land near the river , among the crowd was a figure moving frantically covering his face and the whole stature with a white sheet of cloth he was walking briskly with wide strides . some teen agers were watching him ; one of them was so curious that he went forward to that figure and pulled the white sheet .It fell off and the figure tumbled over falling in the dusty track. His face was covered with dust; It was Deedis. Among the group was Hadjis   , who was surprised to see Deedis covering himself with   that white sheet when only yesterday he was shouting with joy in reaction to the news he heard from the Voice of the Arabs' Ahmad Saeed who was saying : "These are the glad tidings of victory, O Arabs! The enemy airplanes are falling like (zubab' a word that has bad connation in Arabic) flies in Sinai, O Arabs!)"

The refugees and the displaced people were gathered in temporary camp to the east of The Jordan River. It was near the highway to Jerusalem. They lived in tents overcrowded with big families. There were no water. Women had to go the

Eastern Ghour Canal(Yarmouk Canal) to bring water. They carried the buckets of water on their heads. Many children died because of scorpion stings and snake bites. Hunger misery and hardships overwhelmed the whole camp. The miserable condition of the refugees was the bright dawn promised by Deedis and the mobs .who promised the people of victory that would bring about prosperity of a bright dear future.

On the 8th of June, Deedis was over the moon despite the wretchedness and the bitterness of the smashing defeat of the three Arab states. He was shouting: "God is the Greatest, we shall fight! We shall fight!. Many young men gathered around him, he began saying: "Glad tidings,   here you are: the Egyptian people don't admit the defeat; they decided on revenge; they will retaliate. The greatest leader of the nation was about to resign but the people refused. So listen to me! You should join the liberation battalions that shall recover the occupied land from the sea to the river. Tomorrow, you should join the striking forces for liberation of land and man! Deedis and his movement adopted a mitigating terminology in an attempt to alleviate the impact of the unprecedented smashing defeat of the Arabs in 1967. They called the defeat a setback . Deedis and his group would say to the mobs:" great leaders don't win the first battle; the war consists of several battles, and the final battle is the decisive one." They promised the heart–broken humiliated crowds of a battle that would have their chins up. They urged people to be patient and wait for that day.

It was a very hot morning and suddenly there was huge hurricane of sand and severe wind advancing violently from the south. The tents of the camp were as light as fallen leaves.. Many of the tents were carried away, most of the people had their tents blown away by the violent storm. It was very tragic sight, women , children and old men and women were crying. Some children were missing, three children were thrown into the deep water canal and they drowned in the water. A woman was also missing; her husband was shouting her name at the highest pitch of his voice!

The tents for families were A– shaped. The camp was the first camp to be allocated for the refugees and the displaced because it was in a place nearer to the west bank. To the north west of the camp about two kilometers away was a military camp with its white blockbuildings.

The UNRWA (the United Nations Relief and Works Agency for Palestinian Refugees) decided to relief the refugees by providing tents and establishing schools. The camp then was called a temporary camp for refugees, it was near the high way that went from the north to south of the Jordan valley, and it connected the east bank cities with those of the west bank.

At the mountain slope facing the camp in the West Bank about two or three miles west of the river , there was an old Arab military evacuated camp! During the first week following the war, the borders were not monitored. People fleeing their homes in the west bank would pour day and night into Jordan . Bu Ali , one of the chieftains of Munqatta'a, fled his home and he pitched his own tent near the refugee temporary camp. He left his horse loose at night. But when he got up in the next morning, he did not find the horse. He looked for it everywhere, but he could not find it. In the evening some people from Munqatta told him that they saw his horse in the back yard of his house. They tried to get hold of it, but it ran away. The man was moved to tears; he said to the his family members; "You see the horse disdains living away from home ' It is of pure breed.. As the horse went back to the village, let's go home now!?" Therefore, he packed his things, load them on some animals and went home. In the morning he was at home. When the horse recognized him it burst into neighing, welcoming them. It came cantering towards Abu Ali who rubbed her nose and kissed her forefront!

The next morning three children were reported dead, because of yellow scorpion stings. The site of the camp was a habitation of scorpions and serpents.

A lorry came to distribute food and bread. People crowded there, they began competing to get the loaves of bread One of them tumbled Deedis down. He fell down, cursing the man who tumbled him over. Two men came to Deedis and beat him heavily grazing the scalp over his eye brows. Hadjis commented: This is by virtue of your Great leader blessings. Congratulations, cousin, live long and you'll get more of it. Anyway, you are the victorious." You got two loaves of bread from amongst the feet of hungry people!" This is the life your great Leader promised you of. Enjoy it!" Deedis did not say anything, he remained silent!

The most important service for the refugees was education. All the Palestinian people were keen on sending their children to school. The problem was that there was not suitable building for the school. Decision was made to have school for children at the

Temporary camp in multi-room tents pitched up in a space near the main highway. It was near the eastern side of the road .

The students in that school were attracted by the traffic on the high way and the sound of vehicle hooting and noise. One day when the screens of the tents were   rolled up especially the screens of the tents looking west on the road, a bus stopped and a strange figure emerged from the front door of the bus. It was for the first time that people saw this figure. He was wearing a semi-military uniform, He had a well-built stature, the uniform he was wearing had dark green spots and he was wearing a red beret with an eagle emblem glittering. Around his waist was a broad dark green belt with a pistol hanging on his right thigh and two hand grenades attached to it.

His face was stiff and there was a sub-machine rifle in his right hand. None of the students had ever seen a man like that.The man at once jumped to the other side of the road and went rapidly to a banana grove and disappeared among the banana trees.

One day, during the recess time, that man appeared again. He entered the outmost tent at the north end corner of the school site. There were no classes at that time. Some of the students were in the tent. As the man entered the tent, the students started shouting welcome! Welcome!

He reckoned with his right hand indicating for them to be quiet. He greeted them and said;" I am Abu Saffron! A revolutionary member of the Liberation battalions; my duty here is to train you and prepare you for fighting the enemy one day. Our generation as you can see, is still struggling to recover our stolen land. Therefore, We pin our hope on you, for you are the new generation to continue our struggle and free Palestine . You are the victory generation, God willing! The man's, accent sounded like a Bedouin one.

Then, holding the rifle in his right hand with its nozzle up to the sky he said;" This rifle is an eastern bloc-make, it can fire scores of bullets with a few number of men!

The principal suddenly came into the tent; he was very angry and shouted to the man:

"This is not a military camp! How do you dare to come into the school without permission? The gunman raised his hand asking the principal to listen to him:. He said to him firmly: "After what has happened all the rules, regulations and systems, all of them have been broken! With presence of this gun that has the highest sound on earth, no sound should be higher than its sound. Today, a new era has begun, it is the era of the revolutionary law. All laws are under my feet! Do you understand! Go look for them in the west bank. They were left there, in Sinai and the Golan heights. "Now I'm leaving this tent and will never come back , but be sure that you will feel sorry one day!

The principal asked: "Who authorized you to carry out military training here? Our land will not be freed haphazardly. Don't you realize that our site here is exposed to the enemy day and night, what will you do if they spot you now. You do not know that they can spot the ants moving in this camp!"

The gun man said:" I don't care about your   rationality! In short, boys, any one of you who wants to join the revolution can meet me in the banana field! So long!" He took his rifle and hurriedly went out of the tent heading for his base in the banana trees.

At the night of that day, volleys of machine guns were heard buzzing through the air. Trains of red pullets traced the sky above the banana grove through the night.

People in the camp and the nearby village hardly slept that night , some of bullets pierced the tents of the camp and windows of the houses of the nearby village , because the enemy used heavy machine guns. Trains of red bullets were pouring from the west mountains of the river and they landed in the camp and the villages there! In the morning there was a ceasefire. At ten o'clock in the morning life began to go back to normal.

The camp was divided into rectangular blocks with a wide dusty track extending from the east to west separating both blocks.

. On the right angle of the rectangle from the west near the high way, there was huge zinc hut used as a cafe where some young people would meet. At that time, some of the students who refused to go to school were seen to go to that café: they were supposed to meet the gun man there.   Other young men saw the gunman arriving at the café, they went to see what was going on. In fact, the man succeeded in enlisting some if not all of them, especially the young men over seventeen years old. At that time they rejoiced and began dancing, but soon the roar of volleys of machine guns was heard once again, the bullets buzzed through the camp piercing the tents.

Three mortar shells landed on the hut of the cafe which was crowded with people, there was a massacre. At least seven were killed and thirty wounded! There was no school that day, but the next day three officials   told the students to ask their parents to dig trenches and fortify them with whatever material they could afford to stay safely in the trenches.

Muhajer was shocked to see his father very terrified. When the shelling occurred, his father at once went into the trench. He was hiding in. after some time, he wanted to look out of the trench to see what was going; he crept to the opening of the trench and he was shaking like a dry leaf in the wind. The boy was surprised to see him shivering! He said to himself: "At last, the reality proved that this man was phony!" To him, this incident broke the fear barrier that was weighing down on his chest.

He saw that his father who always terrified the members of the whole family: Rifqa and   his brother and sister. They would be terrified of making a mistake that provoked Hadjis . That incident exposed the reality of the ostentatious man. The shelling of the camp smashed the hut and killed some people, but it freed Muhajer of a false belief in Hadjis as the family defender.The Six Day War, the storming of the village and hamlet nearby had not only eradicated the people out of the their land, but it had cleansed the minds of all the villagers of the dreams that haunted their minds about the gallant Arab defenders of the village and the protectors of their families! After the smashing defeat, women tended to reject their husbands' requests and tended not to trust them anymore. The smashing defeat of the Arabs in the war ignited the spark of mutiny in Muhejr's heart . He had been looking for this chance since the day he fled to the gypsies' camp. The incident reinforced his doubts about the insurmountable forte that existed in his mind all the past years. Seeing Hadjis trembling of fear, Muhajer jumped out of the trench and ran into the tent laughing and he said he wanted to bring some water for Hadjis . When he brought the water, Hadjis slapped Muhajer's face twice and said: " the shrapnel of the exploding shell can kill the brave and the coward; recklessness is not heroism. " Rifqa said :" let him do whatever he wants let him die . May Allah fasten the end of his life, let him go to hell!." The boy went out of the hole shouting loudly: "come and see how men   tremble in the trench!" And he began singing singing: The war broke out and

It shook the heart of the weak!

Muhajer's concept of the world has become completely different. The fortes of the whole vast Arab World were only a mirage of the desert sands .The great hallucinations of their great leader who would free the Arab countries from the regressive regimes and his promises of a "new rising bright dear dawn" evaporated in the blitz of the morning of the disgracing Monday, the fifth of June 1967. This defeat not only quenched their pride and dignity, but it also implanted in their hearts hopelessness. it is the unprecedented smashing war that had taken place in such a speed. The progressive pro -Arab commanders should not be trusted any more. The Arab multitudes should no longer believe in the mottos of show-off-war. The people should not buy phony propaganda of the glory of the great phony leader! His image fell to the rock of reality and it was smashed into pieces impossible to fuse again!. Since that date, people started to believe in actions that speak louder than words. The ruler who brought about the eradication of a whole nation from their land had no place on the honor log at all. His name resides in the books of disgrace and humiliation. He is not sacred. His name is listed in the log of the defeated leaders, a fact that cannot be denied forever! In an overnight the Palestinians found themselves in rugged camps by virtue of such a leader who gave priority to his private phony glory based on selfishness. Not only did he tarnish his reputation the Arabation but he also buried the glorious history of the whole nation ; he   threw the glorious history of the Arab-Islamic nation in history garbage dump ! . The Arab multitudes had become distrustful of any propaganda that glorifies the deeds of their phoney rulers.

Muhjaer's images of the strongholds of his father , Hadjis , , of his uncle Dhughayyem. , and the fifteen rural guards of Munqatta'a village ,   all those images had been a mirage in a barren desert ; they disappeared beyond the clouds of the smashing war. He wondered how three of the strongest Arab nations were defeated in less than six days, an unprecedented defeat ever! The wounds had gone deeply into the hearts of the fans of the Great leader. The foe had not defeated the Arabs by his own power. It was the Arabs' weakness that defeated them. They did not plan for the war. The great leader was tapering with the destiny of the all-Arab nation. He subjected himself to the mob whims. He played tricks on them with fiery speeches and inflaming propaganda. Though, he once, in one his speeches, declared that "anyone who tells you he had a plan to free Palestine of the occupation   would be laughing at you!"

The fear barriers were removed forever. The boy concluded that life has other aspects than the explicit ones that the individual may recognize. He said to himself that the victorious invaders should be-little themselves when they recognize that they defeated only the weak leaders ! It as a defeat by chance The invaders should suspect their heroism, in this case! The chance made them victorious.

There must be other dimensions that   exist but there will come a time when they present themselves explicitly. It was hazardous to venture out of the trench. Though,   Muhajer felt some relief. The shelling of the camp put his mind at ease: it liberated him; he thought he could do whatever he wanted. It triggered in him the spark of willpower   .Had the enemy known the positive psychological impact on the mentality of young men of the camp, they would not have bombarded the camp. Every blast gave birth to a wave of determination to encounter the aggression. The bombardment generated self-confidence and will power in the young men who were determined to defend the existence of their people! With blasts taking place in the camp, a new dawn broke and the sun of a new day rose!

The defeat of the Arabs and the bombardment of the camp awakened he the phoenix under the ashes; it shook the dust off itself, forcing its way through the freedom road! The dust of the phony villagers like Dhughayyem , Deedis , Hadjis along with the progressive current , to Muhajer they were no longer defensive castles. Rather , they had collapsed with driving the first wedge into the ground to set up the tents of the refugee camps, when the wind would move the flaps of the tent , the movement of the tent was reminder to Muhajer of the rubbish that he once believed to be strongholds of protection.

On day, Deeds and Dhughayyem saw their sons, Qassim and Qadhi joking in the tent ; Qassim and Qadhi were playing cards in Dhughayyem's tent, they paid no attention the presence of Dhughayyem and Deedis. This indifference upset both fathers. . So simultaneously they both kicked their children out of the tent, each kicking his son respectively. The boys ran away. Dhughayyem and Deedis started throwing stones at them. The two boys ran towards the banana field. There they met the gun man who sent them to training camps outside Jordan!.

At night.a crazy young man   dubbed Bu Zahi went outside the camp to the hill to the north of camp.. The enemy with their powerful light projectors detected him. They sent some flares over the hill , thus lighting the whole area. Instead of hiding , Bu Zahi , ran up a high rock and stood over it shouting : Cheeha Arab , cheeha Arabs."(that is, shame on you,Arabs) . The enemy bombarded the area with three mortar shells the first one of the them ribbed his head off and his corpse was sent rolling down the hill with blood soaking it!

The enemy was unwavering in bombarding the whole Jordan valley. Therefore, a decision was made to evacuate the camp to a safer site far away from the front line.

So, the refugees and the displaced hired trucks and moved to settle in a new camp which was very dusty   at the fringes of the desert.

One, day at the beginning of May,1968, while Hadjis was working with his family in a field of lentils, he was surprised to see his nephew Qassim wearing a camouflaged military uniform with a cap of canvas on his head with the eagle emblem glittering there. He resentfully welcomed his nephew who was a young man about twenty two years of age and asked him about   the   uniform   he was wearing . Qassim answered that it was the uniform of the freedom fighters!

To this, Hadjis commented that he believed that the hand that had woven the uniform was not an Arab hand! The young man laughed and asked: ' How did you know?" Hadjis answered: " simply because I have never seen an Arab wearing like it."

The young man said:" you are right uncle! This suit was made in China and the boots are made in Belgium." He told him that he enlisted as a freedom fighter and promised him that he would free the grove olive he lost in 1967.

He said "It 's high time for the revolutionary work! This youth generation will free the whole land from the sea to the river!"

Hadjis was pleased to hear those words, but he sarcastically said ; " you, be ware of what you're saying. A glory you will not be allowed to attain! There are many obstacles and barricades at the road my son! So be careful of the mines! They may explode at any moment. So keep off the minefields!   You should understand what I mean! You should act wisely!"

Muhajer was pleased to see his cousin who promised to recover the lost land. Muhajer happily said :" Take me with you ' I can help! I am no longer a little child! Take me with you now I am a man, now I am almost seventeen ! look I have strong muscles and I am taller than you."Hadjis got angry and said: " you have to finish your schooling. The only hope for the refugees is to finish schooling when you grow up you can do whatever you like! The boy said:" now we are in the recess period; there is no school for three months June, July and August . Let   me go with him and try! If I liked it I will continue. "The young man said to his uncle:" let him go, and I'll take care of him!" Hadjis refused saying "His elder brother has enlisted in the Army, and now you want to take this child! Go away and let me not see your face here again!."

Rifqah intervened: "Let him go to hell , we scarified the elder son to keep this wicked boy . Let him go so that we get rid of him! At least we will save the expanses of his food and clothing!."

Hadjis said : " This is the first time you speak wisely! Qassim take care of him! Pay attention to him. let him not accompany the dishonest persons ! You know what I mean."

The young man said:" Don't worry, uncle! We don't have such persons in our lines!"

Hadjis : " don't tell me! I know the reality, the other day I saw a gay, I mean it, who was wearing a chain with bullet.

He was wearing a T- shirt with a photo of his comrade Lenin. Those people will not do anything good in the interest of our cause!

In the evening, Muhajer left with his cousin to his base which was in the mountains that looked on the west bank. They arrived at midnight,. The boy did not know where he was.

Qassim   took Muhajer to the commander of the base and told him that the boy was his cousin and he wanted to train him in the base. He assured him that the boy was good for the base because he knew the topography of the land and the way to the western mountains where the old hamlet was. Muhajer was surprised to see that the principal of Munqatta'a school was the commander of the base , but he was pleased . The commander welcomed him and encouraged him to avail himself as he knew him to be a good student and he hoped that he would be a good fighter. In two weeks' time, the boy was able to use the rifle and hand grenades well! The following week, a patrol was to go into the occupied land to send some material there. The rendezvous point was Hadjis 's grove. It was a proper place for storing the material in the cavern therein. The cavern was difficult to spot because it was covered by dense flora and a lot of trees around it. When the patrol reached its destination, none of them was able to locate the cavern except Muhajer who took them directly to there. There was much grass growing there and the flora also covered the opening of the cave. The place had not been weeded for almost two years! The dense high grass covered the opening of the cavern completely. So the patrol members began uprooting and cutting the grass to find the entrance   and they found the entrance of the dark cavern. The commander of the patrol said the entrance of the cave might be spotted easily by the enemy . Therefore, nobody should sleep there! The patrol had to leave the place and sleep in another place , but before leaving they had to cover the entrance with turf   to camouflage   it . Muhajer said that he preferred to sleep under the carob tree he and his family used to stay under in Summer. Qassim went with him: one would sleep while the other would guard him. When the watch man got tired the sleeping one would get up and guard him. So commander finally decided that all members of the patrol would sleep therein but sentinels would be appointed .It was agreed that they would not stay at day in the cave. They should leave the place and hide in a huge carob tree that had thick foliage sprouting from ground to its top .The tree looked as if it were a forest by itself, it had a thick undergrowth that all of the eight men of the patrol were able to hide therein. The commander went round the tree while his men were hiding there in and made sure that they were hidden completely.

It was around ten o'clock in a sunny morning when two huge helicopters flew over and landed on the flat opening adjacent the carob tree where the patrol men were hiding. One of the two charters landed not far away from the tree. It was roaring loudly with a deafening roaring. The branches at the top of the tree began to sway violently and they hit one another. The commander of the patrol ordered his men to be prepared for an engagement. So all of them were ready, with fingers at the triggers. All the members of the patrol thought that the boy with them would cry , but he proved to them that he was a man with a high stamina; he was brave that he remained silent and ready for the engagement.

The charter with its huge tube and giant rotors that were rotating violently came to silence. A few minutes later; the charter's rear door was opened and soldiers came out with full battle dress and armed to teeth with machine guns, automatic rifles…etc.

They fell in three lines; that were about fifty soldiers, men and women. . Their commander ordered them to turn right and march forward: they were heading for the carob tree. When they were just twenty meters away from the carob tree the commander of the patrol asked his men to fire when he himself opens fire. One of the pattrol members that he would not fire because he was afraid that his bullets might kill the beautiful women. The othr members laughed timidly . But a few minutes later, the enemy commander ordered his soldiers to halt and he ordered them to fall out, every two soldiers went together. A few minutes later, the whole force disappeared in the groves, but the commander and the captain of the charter and two men went and sat inside the charter! The crackle of their walky-talky was heard by the patrolmen. As the soldiers were moving towards the carob tree. , a few swallows flew and perched on the branches of the tree. But the most dangerous moment was when a dog came yelping and thrust itself into the tree among the patrolmen. Qassim was about to shoot him thinking that it belonged the charter's force ,but the commander snatched the rifle from him. The dog was horrified by roaring of the charter's engine. Therefore, he stood outside the carob tree and began barking. One of the patrol men   whispered that "the dog will expose us; he is going to give us to the enemy as presents." At that moment, the dog attracted the attention of the charter's commander. He came out of the charter carrying something in his hand and hurried towards the dog. When he was a few meters away from

the dog, he threw to him what he was carrying. The dog went
happily and began helping himself to it. It was piece of canned
beef, the patrolmen reckoned.

The area was ablaze with bullets, the soldiers were combing the area with their machine guns and rifles. They rained every thick bush with bullets, they threw hand grenades in the empty caves and cisterns Everything was attacked in the groves; every single tree, every single hole or even the hand-made wells for collecting water were blasted. The carob tree that hid the patrol was not attacked , because it was nearer to the charter .

In the sky ,there were two aircraft fighters supporting the ground force . The hills towards the south of Hadjis ' s grove were machine gunned by the two aircrafts.

The tension lasted four hours. At two o'clock in the afternoon the soldiers came back to the charter, fell in line and the commander started calling them one by one. When the last soldier went into the charter , two soldiers came out and burst into shouting the name of a missing solders:" Yaffo". One of the charters took off and flew to Wazeer hamlet.

A few minutes later , Yaffo appeared laming ; it seemed that he was bitten by a snake as he was holding with his hand a snake that he had killed . The charter took off, and the men of the patrol were relieved and all of them began commending the boy who showed high stamina and bravery. When the sun set behind the mountains, darkness began to weigh down. There appeared something like two ghosts. They were approaching the sheep shepherd who had his sheep sleep in the area where the two charters had landed. It was a woman armed with a Carl Gustav M/45 submachine gun. She brought food to the patrol. She told him to ask the patrol to leave, because the soldiers of the enemy told the inhabitants of the hamlet that they were sure that some men were hiding in the area and they would come to comb the area every day. And she told the shepherd to tell patrol that the material had been sent to its destination and thus their task was accomplished. The enemy commander told the villagers in the hamlet that the day after tomorrow, they would search the area again to find the hiding terrorists as he said. Therefore, the patrol had to leave at once.

It was after mid night when the patrol reached the river. They had to cross the river swimming. They accompanied two men whom they brought from the west bank: those men were not good at swimming .

A few days later, the base commander summoned Muhajer and told him the general commander was pleased when heard of his bravery. Therefore, he ordered that "the youth like you should have courses of religion education. This meant that the young people like Muhajer should go the base of the shakes (scholars) who were supposed to give the course needed." The next day the boy carried his bag and went to the Shakes' base. There was a huge old oak tree and there were twenty young men sitting around a shake! the shake's face was familiar to Muhajer! It rang a bell in his mind. He remembered his name: It was Abu Ibrahim who was dubbed Museired at Munqata'a village because he would tell flagrant lies!

The boy thought him the shake who was supposed to give the young men the course. He hurried to the seminar, greeted the men and nervously said :" listen guys ! I know this man and he knows me well! But let me tell you something: Frankly if I knew that there were a person who told more flagrant lies than I do except my uncle Museireid , I would kill myself at once!"All the men there burst into laughing!

Then a man with a long grey beard hurried to the place and asked what was going on. Therefore, he got angry with Muhajer and said that he could not absorb him there in his base; but Bu Ibrahim said that he knew the boy and his parents and begged the commander to forgive him!

Two days later, the deputy-commander of the revolutionary forces in the region arrived at the Shakes' base. He said that he came to check the conditions and wanted to meet Muhajer, the boy who proved that he was braver than many youth of his age!

The Commander of the base, the shake with the grey long beard, said that he gave him leave for a week and added that the boy was undisciplined and he should not stay at the base with respectable men! The deputy- Commander said: "when he reports back next week, take him at once to the cavern, my head quarter, I will look into the matter and take a decision."

Then he added: "by the Way, tell me brother Bu Khalid ! what 's the story with sheep bowels ; it seems that many of your men are suffering from diarrhea; You promised that you will set the whole occupied land ablaze under the feet of the occupying forces . But I clearly see that you have gained weight and you can hardly move, it seems to me that you are struggling with eating too much mutton and bowels of sheep!" Bu Khalid said with a harsh voice but firmly:" listen deputy-commander ! I do respect you, but my role here is more important than fighting in the field. You know that you assigned me here to educate the brothers: I teach them how to be pious and behave decently according the principles of Islam.The Commander said : " viva ,viva . You want to spoil all that we have been struggling for, you want to take us 1300 years back, to hell with you and your principles!" To this Shake Bu Khalid said: "then tell me, what the religion of your organization is! The deputy answered with a sarcastic smile on his lips: "Our organization has no religion! We believe in all religions, the earthy ones and the celestial ones, we are opportunists! Are you pleased?"

Bu Khalid said; "Then don't blame us, since you have no religion, we shall leave you and look for another people who have religion .So long."

The Shake shouted to his people: " O men, come and listen to these people you are fighting under their leadership. They say that they have no religion! So pack your things and let's leave at once!"

Two days later the shakes' base was evacuated , none of them had ever been seen among revolutionary forces!

Muhajer had a leave for week and he spent seven days in the dusty camp for refugees . The camp was among the fields of lentils and wheat. In the afternoon, the east south wind would blow bringing with it clouds of dust and if the wind was Violent it would play havoc with the camp: Tents were carried away, tin huts were blown away also! Life was impossible in that camp!

. It was impossible to eat decently. The most dangerous things were the rattle snakes that would creep into the tents and sleep under the billows ,if any.

At night, the most remarkable thing was seeing the red volleys of sub- machine guns tracing through the sky over the camp tents .

One night a lot of red bullets were streaming through darkness in the sky! There was a dancing party for a revolutionary guy. There were a lot of revolutionaries who came to take part in the dancing. The bridegroom's tent was pitched at the south end of the camp and there was a wide flat piece of land;

the soil was dry and it was milled into dust powder. Many of his revolutionary comrades came to take part in the dabkah or dancing, all of them were armed to teeth wearing their full battle dress. The bridegroom was dubbed 'The Mule'. He was good at playing the flute for the dancing. He was a short guy, slim with big head with wide eyes and hooked nose, his face face was black and his hair was curly and untidy.. He was good at playing the flute. He would play long hours without getting tired.

There was a person singing revolutionary songs. Moved by the words of the singer, the guys with rifles would shoot volleys of red tracers in the dark night. Moreover, some would throw sound hand grenades into the dry gutter adjoining the tents. There were stunning explosions that many small children bursts into crying of fear. The Mule, after playing continually the flute for several hours, got tired and he was out of breath. He stopped playing the flute. A revolutionary with his giant body hurried to The Mule and shouted to him: "continue playing!" He cuffed The Mule's neck several times. The Mule got nervous; he said loudly:" Leave me alone . I give up getting married. I don't want to get married." A group of his friends hurried to him. The party was over and everybody went home! The enthusiastic revolutionary men threw four sound grenades into the gutter. They exploded loudly with white smoke going up in the sky. Nobody in the camp was able to sleep that night!

While the party was going in, Rifqa was alone in the tent, the children and their father went see the party. Muhajer noticed that his sister, brother and Hadjis their father were at the party. He went back to the tent of his family, he found his mother, Rifqa staying there by herself. So he went into the tent directly. he drew the bolt handle of his k47 sub machine gun , he said: " listen , Mother , I've addressing you "mother" for all my life with you, for more than twenty years , but whenever I addressed you s, you would say to me: son of the perished ; you would curse me! You hated me all the time. You often said to me that you are not my mother though you fed me from your breast ; you always humiliated me. Now, I am asking you to tell me the truth. Tell me the truth! Otherwise, I 'll kill you and kill myself ,too.. He pointed the nozzle of the rifle to her head!!

Rifqa thought for a while and said ; ' listen you are a grown up man now! But I am afraid that you won't believe me!"

He said: "Tell me the truth , I am not a little boy who would believe any ting .: Hadjis who was to me   castle or majestic temple   that gave me shelter. I used to fear him and at the same time I thought that he was able to protect me from the beasts of the wilderness and the criminal teacher in my first year of school. I felt secure when he shot the two hyenas, but I felt insecure when he took to me the grove and beat me heavily there!"

He added:"Now, I realize that this life is a waste journey and all the castles I trusted them for protection and thought they were strongholds that would safeguard my existence all those castles have collapsed in the dark the moments we fled our village like wet hens. The great leader himself was once to me a stronghold,   but he collapsed in a moment , nothing remains except this rifle , the rifle of revolution ! Now tell me; I have been accustomed to shocks; don t be afraid you will remain my mother, though!"

At that moment Rifqa said: 'Do you remember when I told you that we found you in the heath where the gypsies left you? I was kidding with you! But the fact is bitter than that, it is buried in the cavern of the grove we lived in! It was a cavern haunted by your mother's spirit!"

Muhajer said :" Then, you are not my real mother ! Who are you?" Rifqa answered: "listen: as you know we used to live in that cavern in winter; the cavern was divided into three compartments . The first compartment was at the entrance of the cavern. It was wider than the other two compartments. It was wider enough that would take in twenty people sitting on mattresses , because it was the area that was not stinky as the other compartments of the cavern . We used to live with the children there!

The middle compartment was a store for grain and other things while the deepest one was a store for the threshed straw and it was a feeding place for the cow , the donkey and the mule that were tied at night in that place.

One night at the end of January, it was a very cold; rain fell as sleet. Therefore, we kindled a big fire with a lot of logs to warm the cavern. At mid night as we were going to sleep, a ghost appeared in the first compartment. The ghost was wearing white dress from head to foot, it was dark, but the fire in the cavern was weak. It was difficult to see clearly. So Hadjis held his rifle and fired two bullets towards the ghost. It fell down immediately to the ground with a faint cry!

Then,we lit a bonfire and Hadjis went to the falling ghost. It turned out that it was a woman who was bleeding heavily. Her blood was like a stream ; but she was not dead. When we realized that she was a woman, I sat down near her body ,putting her head on my knee. I asked her who she was. She said that she was a refugee who quarreled with her husband and his mother asked him to divorce her. She was chs out of home and went looking for her family she lost her way in the darkness. When she noticed the light of the fire she decided to go there to spend the night there! The woman was in her last moments of life she fainted and never recovered!

At that night we could not sleep: I had a son who was about three weeks of age . I had him sleep in a canvas cradle which was hung at both ends with steel wedges driven into the wall of the cavern. As the child did not move I went to his cradle and found out it was dead, for one of bullets hit its head and the baby died at once. I began crying, but Hadjis hurried to a bundle thrown by the corpse of women and he found out that there was a baby of the same age as our child's age! We were in an ordeal, if the folks of woman found out that Hadjis killed her, they might kill him or sue him. And he might be sent prison for many years.

The woman passed away; Hadjis told me that what he did was a crime and he would be jailed or the folk of the woman might kill him in revenge of her. He said that if the baby in the bundle was a boy, the solution was easy. It turned out that it baby was a boy . Hadjis was pleased, but my heart was heavy with sadness for the loss of my own son. I lived all my life lamenting his loss. I believed that I lost my son because of you and your mother. That is why hated you. I considered you a bad omen to me!

In the morning. It snowed heavily covering all the foot prints of people or nimals that walked on the first layer of snow . The snow helped us hide the secret of the killed woman whose footprints were covered by the new layer of snow falling on that area;it was very thick especially in the grove and the hills and dales around it.

As we were living in Isolation in that place and nobody would have noticed that woman coming to us , we decided to keep the matter secret. Hadjis asked me not tell anybody about it. He said that we would take the baby instead of the boy we lost. Hadjis , with my help, dug a grave for the woman and the baby in the third compartment; he buried both-your mother and my son together there and covered the top of the grave with threshed hay to conceal it and let the animals sleep over it. He buried her bundle with her and everything that was with her: money rings: earrings and jewels. We gave you the name of Muahjer, our son's ." she continued:

" No body have ever known that secret except you now.! Three weeks later my sister came to visit us in the cavern. She said she wanted see the baby, my second son that I gave birth to six weeks ago and she had helped me give birth to him!

She went to the cradle and noticed that the complexion of the baby was different from that of our real son. I said to her that infants keep changing complexions from month to month!

She said that the baby had been changed and she believed that we exchanged it with a gypsy baby, because she realized the baby was whiter: Gypsies had white and blonde faces! She started laughing and said:" you might have borrowed it from a blonde woman" . One more thing, she said that the baby did not resemble Hadjis who was as black as an eggplant ! When she   stopped talking   Hadjis came in the cavern and my sister had to leave.

.

Muhajer was moved to tears . and with a choked voice said :" I have lived in misery all my life :tormented , scolded, and cursed!" why? What was my fault? What was my fault?   Why have you treated me like that! You should have treated me as a real son. Did not you feed me from your breast? The milk that nurtured my bones was yours. I am your son! Had I not been there, you would have all suffered, Hadjis would have been jailed or executed for the crime! Your existence as a family was pinned on my existence with you. Imagine your destiny without me! What would have happened to you if I had not been there all that time? The secret of your crime would have been known!

Now you are all for me collapsing castles. Even the family has collapsed. Selfishness had spoiled my life. All people whom I thought to be castles protecting me are now collapsing in front of me. My life has been a straying journey and you all for me are collapsing castles. Nothing is sacred for me from now on, even life itself. This earthy life that enslaves us I'll put an end to it. A body that enslaves me soon I will free myself out of it. I shall dig the bones of my mother out to verify your story.   Now, I venture my life for the Truth, see you in hell!

At that moment he heard somebody calling him. He hurried out of the tent to see Bu Ibrahim in front of him. He asked: "what's wrong Bu Ibrahim?."

Bu Ibrahim hesitated and said :" bad news, your cousin was trapped in a mine field in the west bank, he is in hospital in the nearby city. You should go and see him. The base jeep is still here, you can ask the driver to take you there to see him. So Muhajer quickly brought his rifle and hurried to the **jeep**. In the morning he got to the hospital and went directly to the room of his cousin.When Muhajer saw Qassim, he did not recognize him at first: His face was completely spotted with pellets of black dry blood. Qassim with a faint voice called him.

Muhjaer lent over Qassim's head and said: "Is that you ,Qassim ?

Qassim said : "Yes! Yes!"

He was covered with white bed sheets and was not a able to move his arms that were both bandaged but the blood soaked both bandages. This aroused Muhajer's curiosity. He lifted up the sheet off the bed but he was shocked. Qassim's right leg was amputated . A few inches of it remained below the knee!

Muhjaer shouted : " O, my God No! No! No!" Then Qassim reckoned to him with his right hand fingers which appeared from beneath the white bandage to come and sit on a chair near him. Qassim said with difficulty : " Don't cry my dear! It's my fate! We have to sacrifice our souls not only parts of our bodies! I pride on my wounds!"

Then Muhajer asked how it happened! Qassim chokingly said: "As you know we had been preparing for this operation for six weeks. We were 18 persons, We were supposed to go to point 222 and fetch a collaborator who guided the enemy to the place of our brothers Qadhi and his friends who fell martyrs in our groves ! We left the base after the sunset. We headed to ford 421; it is a shallow crossing point and we crossed it easily! Before we reached the ford, When we were at the milled area by the bridge to the east north of the army camp. One of our comrades said that he would dance the dabkah in the flat milled open area to south of the bridge at the foot of the mound there. As it was screened by the lope of a small hill, the open area was hidden from the enemy light projectors.   That brother said that he believed he would not come back alive; he was going to die that time. So the guys spent about an hour dancing and then headed for the river, when we got to the ford , the enemy garrison 522 was exchanging fire with the Arab army point there to the east of the river.   Therefore, we crossed the river easily and safely as the enemy soldiers were hiding in their shelters during the skirmish !

When going through the flat plain to the south of 522 , We were walking in diagonal line. I was at the head of the line which was slanted to the right. So we were moving slowly and suddenly I heard explosions at the rear end of the line. I thought the enemy point 521   was firing at us . Therefore I turned to the left in order to go back,   I opened fire in the direction of point 521 which was far away from me and started to go back   , but the explosions were going on. Suddenly I found myself flying high in the sky. There was white smoke before my eyes! I glimpsed it in the darkness as I was swaying in the air. Then I fell heavily to the ground . I did not feel any pain at that time . I fell in a deep wide crater made by one of the blasts , so I stood up swiftly , but my right side was not as tall as my left one; I lost balance. So I fell down with my heavy load of about fifty kilograms into the crater again . But this time I fell on the shattered broken bone of my right leg.   It was shattered by the mine and it was slanted as if it were a knife. When I fell to the ground I leaned to the right because my right leg was shorter than the left which was intact so the broken bone of my right leg went through the ground; I felt a terrible pain that I lost consciousness.   I remained unconscious in the hole for some time, but I began   feel pain as I was reviving. It was difficult for me to breathe, it was the death rattle. I was bleeding heavily , but I tried to bandage my wound with the torn canvass ; it was useless. I felt the heavy burden which was in a canvass bag on my back. With difficulty I got rid of it and began   to climb out of the hole. I began creeping to the east. As I was creeping , my left leg tumbled over with Salah , my friend , he asked me not to leave him , he   clung to my left leg with his hand ,but a few minutes later his hand fell off my leg , I realized that he passed away. Then I continued creeping towards the east. I wanted to reach the bank of the river , because I was afraid the soldiers of the enemy might   arrive and take me a prisoner. Then I tumbled over with a another one; he was Salem   ,   but he was already dead . Then I crept further. Suddenly I heard   a movement among the high dry grass; and two figures were approaching me: I held out my revolver pointing towards them and called out: "who is there?" , the answer was: "friend don't fire!"

I asked or the watch word ! I know that they were from the supporting team! When they reached me they tried to carry me, but *I* insisted that they   move the bodies of my friends first. They called   another group and   evacuated us to the east. While they were carrying me across the river I fell in the water and the cold water of the river helped stop my bleeding. I lost nearly all my blood;. The doctors say they will look for the type of my blood which is O+ . Muhjaer said said that his blood type was O+. He went to the blood bank where he donated a unit of blood for his cousin. Then he came back to him.

Qassim said he was not sorry for what had happened to him : he said it was a punishment by God for horrible acts: one was when he was a boy of seventeen; when he broke the wings of the little hawks that his father ordered him to return them to their nest on a high rock. Muhajer , said : I remember that very well . it was a dark night , when we went to visit you in that remote mountain we were three: Faruq and you and I. you climbed up the rock and took the four birds down of the nest.

They were about to leave the nest in two or free weeks, but uncle Dhughayyem ordered you to return them to their nest. When we got to the nest it was high on the rock, you could climb up and put them there ,but you broke both wings of each one them and threw them above the rock towards the nest. For sure, they died. Qassim said:

"I molested a girl and she invoked god to break my legs! "Muhajer said " repent your sins and return to Allah ; he will forgive you! now' I have to leave . I am going to the base and will go back tomorrow to our grove to bring the revolver I forgot there when we went there last time six months ago! We might not meet again. They kissed each other good-by!

MUhajer went his base ,he arrived there at night . He went directly to his iron bed which was under a tree and went to sleep. In the morning he took his rifle and some magazines for it; they were stuffed with ammunition . He left the base heading west. He spent the day in the citrus groves in the Jordan valley . When the darkness weighed down he knew the ford he would cross,. When he got there a skirmish erupted between the enemy forces and theArab army point in the east bank   ; they began exchanging fire with position 552 which was not far away from the crossing ford. The enemy soldiers did not notice him as they were engaged or hiding in their shelters. So he crept through stream of water pouring it water into the river. So he crept up he stream passing beneath the barbed wire without any need to cut the wires. He was able to avoid the mines set there. He located them by using a dry cell pen torch. He saw that there were two personnel mines. He raised his feet one after another and passed safely over them.

When he left the place he began walking on the basalt stones scattered in the area , and he was able to reach a deep valley which went directly to the grove . In the afternoon he reached the cavern in the grove. He took a rest for fifteen minutes, he took Hadjis 's old shovel and a pick axe that were kept in the cavern. He started digging, after some time , he reached the skeleton of his real mother . With tears running down his cheeks, he opened the canvass bag buried with her, . There were some documents; among them was a birth certificate for him:

The child's name: Mussafer   Father's name: saber family Name : Kureitat

Mother's name : Huda

Place of birth: Nakhlah village

Date of Birth 1/1/19551

Muhajer at last was able to find his identity. He was the son of real family who was deeply rooted in that Holy Land! Now, he would stay there for ever. He was determined to stay in the cavern with the bones of his mother in peace and he hoped to be buried in his mother's grave.

Muhajer wept bitterly , but when he lamed down he felt awve of relief over whelming him. At last he he realized whyhe was tromentd and despised. Twenty years of humialtiona nd mal treatment because he had no identity. Now ,ensuring that he had ad identity , hw would never care about any storm. He would face all kind of aggression and oppression , once the individual realizes that he ahs an identity , hwill never ar about all the challenges of life. The cav for him as of that point of time has become the source of confidence. There his roots are deeply roo rooted . he could feel the soul of his mother enveloping him with compassion ; he felt safe there.

He said to himself: "I shall never leave this place. No power on earth shall eradicate me from here. Here I will live and die but my soul will always be here!

www.ingramcontent.com/pod-product-compliance
Lightning Source LLC
Chambersburg PA
CBHW061539120726
48001CB00004B/1625